EDANE

Immortal Highlander, Clan Mag Raith Book 3

HAZEL HUNTER

HH ONLINE

Hazel loves hearing from readers!
You can contact her at the links below.

Website: hazelhunter.com

Facebook:
business.facebook.com/HazelHunterAuthor

Newsletter: HazelHunter.com/news

I send newsletters with details on new releases, special offers, and other bits of news related to my writing. You can sign up here!

Chapter One

A FINE MIST of rain greeted Edane mag Raith as he led his restless chestnut gelding out of the stable. He flipped his tartan over the quiver and bow at his shoulder to keep both dry. The storm rushed over Dun Chaill in a vast river of gray cloud, parting now and then to allow brief flashes of daylight. They came from the sun, now as a golden bauble surfacing and submerging in the roiling tempest.

Aye. He felt the storm reaching inside him, stirring the change that came only with the wind and rain. *Take me with you.*

Domnall mag Raith came to join him, and surveyed the skies with his shrewd verdant eyes. Tall, broad and heavily muscled, the chieftain dwarfed all but one of his clan.

"I'd ride with you," Domnall said, "but I vowed to Jenna I'd finish the bath chamber today."

"'Tis a patrol of the boundary. Likely the Gods shall but give me and the nag a good wash." Edane swung up onto the gelding, and scanned the storm once more before regarding the chieftain. "Yet if they drop a naked lass in my lap, I'll be longer away."

Domnall grinned and stepped back. "Then I bid you fair hunting, Brother."

The gelding went still as Edane let the storm transform him. Each time he had made the change he imagined he'd feel accustomed to it, but the electric thrill of becoming lighter than air still sizzled through his veins. Brilliant light engulfed him as he touched his heels to the horse's sides, and his mount surged forward. A moment later the gelding's hooves left the ground as they soared up into the clouds.

Edane and the other Mag Raith had quickly learned that their ability to fly came only with a storm. During their first ascent, while battling the Sluath, they had been astounded to discover they could fight their enemy in the air. The winged underworld demons that had long ago enslaved the five hunters had apparently given them the ability, along with other bewildering alterations. The Mag Raith no longer aged or grew sick, and even the gravest wounds they sustained healed rapidly. Each hunter also had a particular power beyond that of an ordinary mortal. How and why the demons had bestowed such gifts remained a mystery, for the Sluath had also stripped the hunters of their memories.

Edane still resented many things the Sluath had done to him and his brothers, but not this. Flying through the lashing rain and howling wind made him feel as he did with a bow in his hands: strong and sure.

Now looking down on the sprawling walls and towers of Dun Chaill, a sense of accomplishment added to Edane's elation. Left to rot for centuries, the castle had been in ruins when the Mag Raith had arrived to claim it. After the many months he and his clan had spent rebuilding and restoring the keepe, it was beginning to look more like a proper stronghold.

The feel of nearby magic sparkled against his flesh and drew Edane's attention back to the air before him, where he could see the shimmer of the looming spell boundary. He didn't know who had placed the protective enchantment around Dun Chaill and the surrounding forests, but the ancient spell caster had been very powerful. The ward had protected the ruins so closely that not even the smallest insects could cross the spell barrier.

But the Sluath may.

He remembered the lone scout that had attacked the stronghold during another storm. Domnall had slain the demon before it could summon the rest of its infernal horde, but the suddenness of the attack had prompted the chieftain to begin storm patrols.

The mist below Edane parted, and he frowned as he spotted a pale figure running through the tall grasses of the glen. The only mortals near Dun Chaill had burned and abandoned their village in the spring after what Domnall surmised was an outbreak of plague. This one appeared to be a lad, perhaps left behind to die but now recovered.

His gaze shifted to the flashing light in the clouds behind the boy, from which a Sluath demon descended. Since the demons preyed on mortals left alone and vulnerable, his pursuit could mean only one fate for the lad.

Edane urged his mount to descend. He reached back to fling aside his tartan as he drew an iron-tipped arrow from his quiver, letting the bow slide down into his fist.

"You'll no' steal this one, you fack."

※

IF THE GORGEOUS goon with the wings grabbed her, Nellie Quinn knew she'd be cut down like cheap hooch. She'd figured that out the minute she'd eyeballed him swooping in from the clouds, all icy claws and teeth.

"Rebel slut," the goon had hissed. "You'll make a fine prize for our prince."

Whatever big cheese he worked for, Nellie knew he was some kind of button man, so she ran. Now a Robin Hood riding the sky on a horse was coming at her from the other direction, a bow in his hand.

"Oh, swell."

She swerved away, ducking as she did. She heard a whistle and glanced back to see Robin clip the goon with three arrows, one after another, so fast she only saw them hit.

The goon screeched and nearly fell to the ground. Black stuff splashed from his wings as he flapped and lunged back up to disappear into the clouds. Nellie promptly tripped and fell, pain streaking up from her ankle as she flopped into a puddle.

I'm done running.

She rolled over and let the rain wash the mud from her face. The rest of her got a good, cool dousing, too, which was when she realized she was in the altogether. She pushed herself up on her elbows to be sure, and saw Robin Hood running toward her.

Nellie should have tried to crawl off, but she was too busy enjoying the show. Golly, but he was handsome. Wet scarlet hair poured around a Valentino face. He had eyes so blue they should have been July sky. All that long, keen body made her hands itch to pet him.

The only thing she didn't like were the weird black tattoos on his right arm. Something about them made her want to spit.

He can cover them up, Nellie thought, enchanted.

"Lad, arenae you—"

As he got close, he stopped and stared at her bare peaches and kitty.

Not that she had much fruit or fur to show, she thought, and then chuckled with relief. She had what she had, and the goon didn't have her, and that was jake, all because of Robin.

"Not a fella," she said. To show she still had some manners, she held out her hand. "Nellie Quinn. Thanks for drilling that goon. Thought for a minute there I was headed for the big sleep."

"My name's Edane mag Raith."

Rather than shake, he tugged the wet green and black blanket from his shoulders and knelt down to cover her with it.

Delighted to have him so close, Nellie curled a hand around his neck, and tugged him forward to give him a quick kiss. He tasted like rain and man, and he smelled even better, so she went back for another, longer try. Oh, what she'd give for a room and a bed and all the time in the world with Edane. He kept his eyes open like hers, but after a bit she realized he wasn't kissing her back.

No point getting stuck on a fella who didn't want her. With a sigh she broke it off.

"Why did you that?" he asked, his breath caressing her lips.

"You saved me." She traced a finger across his pretty mouth. He sure did talk funny, but he was just too sheik for her not to crush on. "So, you got a squeeze back at your joint, or can a girl hope?"

He blinked. "The demon didnae chase you from Wachvale."

"Don't know. I came to, saw the flash and claws, and heard him say something about a prize and a prince. I skedaddled." Strange things flashed through her mind as she wrapped his drippy plaid around her and sat up. "Feeling a bit out on the roof here, Danny. Give me a hand up?"

"No' Danny," he said. "Edane."

"Right." Boy, was he a stickler. As soon as Edane took hold of her, the images faded.

Instead Nellie felt something like a hot kiss on the back of her neck, and swiped at it. "Hey, that smarts." She traced the heated marks with her fingertips. "Like something burned me."

Edane stepped behind her, removed her hand, and then made a funny sound. A moment later he came around again, and looked at his arm before he met her gaze.

"You're marked by the Sluath."

"Yeah, sure." She smiled. "What's a Sluath?"

"More than I've time to tell you." He nodded toward the big copper-colored horse. "We must now go, my lady."

"Before that goon buzzes back, right?" Relieved to know he wouldn't ditch her there, Nellie tucked her arm through his. "Let's breeze."

Walking up to the flying horse should have given Nellie the jitters, but the minute she got close she saw the big beast didn't come with wings. The animal also seemed oddly familiar to her, as if she'd been around plenty of bang-tails before this one.

"Heya, Houdini." She offered a hand,

which the horse sniffed and nuzzled, instantly charming her. "Aren't you the sweetest?"

"Forgive me my haste, my lady," Edane said, hoisting her onto the strange saddle as if she were made of feathers. He mounted behind her and tucked a strong arm around her waist, sending a wave of heat through her middle. "We must fly."

A cloud of light swamped Nellie, making her tingle all over, and then the horse galloped up into the air. Her wet hair whipped around her cheeks as she looked down at the ground dwindling beneath them. She hadn't imagined any of it. The guy had a flying horse.

She definitely wasn't ossified. This was really happening to her.

"'Twillnae take long to reach the stronghold," he called to her through the wind rushing around them. "Dinnae fear."

"You slay me," she yelled back, leaning against his hard chest with a shivery shimmy. It felt so good to be pressed up against him as they soared through the sky she laughed like a kid. "I'm sitting so pretty that I'm never climbing down."

His hand spread over her side, his fingers

not too tight now. Next, he'd start roaming them around and having fun with her, Nellie thought, sure she wouldn't mind that. A little petting might just do the trick to clear out the cobwebs. Only he didn't. Nellie covered his hand with hers to give him a nudge in the right direction, and he curled his fingers through hers. The affectionate move made a funny pang bounce around in her chest.

He could have pawed me all he wanted back in the grass. Instead he's getting me safe. He's just like…

Nellie yelped as a shiv of pain rammed through her head. At the same time the cloud dropped a burst of heavy rain over them, soaking her all over again.

Edane leaned closer to say, "Nearly home, my lady."

"Swell."

She let her pounding head fall back against his shoulder and closed her wet eyes. Even as cold and drenched as she was, being in his arms felt better than trying to think. She didn't know anything more than this, and that felt good. For a little while she could just pretend she was his girl, and let the bucketing torrents wash her clean.

Too bad the storm couldn't do that to all the dark blankness on the inside of her head. She must have really done it up last night to have such a hangover.

The horse whinnied just before it landed, and rain tears streaked down Nellie's face as she rubbed her eyes. When she could see again, she stared at the tumbled-down stones and decaying towers in front of them and blinked a few times.

Nope, it wasn't getting better.

"Jeepers, Danny," she said as he dismounted. "Your joint's a dump." She caught how he was looking at her and recalled how huffy he'd gotten about using his proper name. "Edane, sorry."

"'Tis called Dun Chaill, no' a joint." He sounded perplexed rather than annoyed. "I live here with my brothers, the Mag Raith, and their mates." Taking hold of her waist, he swung her down off the saddle. "You'll be safe here, my lady."

Okay, so his place wasn't the duck's quack. Nellie was more interested in how her new fella intended to keep her safe. He liked her, judging by the way he held her against him just a little too long before setting her on her feet. Every bit of him was hard and tough, and made her want to ditch the plaid and feel him against all of her naked skin, right here.

"The rain doesnae stop." He stared at her mouth as if he'd never seen one, and his hands tightened a little on her waist. "We should go in."

"Or we could just go." She tugged at one of the worn hide strips lacing the top of his shabby shirt together. A guy this sheik should be dressed in the best, not in duds a hobo would burn.

"Go where?" Edane murmured.

"Maybe back to my place." Thing was, Nellie couldn't remember her place, or where it was, exactly. Trying to think about it just made her head hurt again. "Where have I got to, anyway? Jersey?"

His fascination with her kisser ended right there.

"You've come to Scotland, my lady," Edane said, folding his long fingers over hers. "Come inside now. My clan shall welcome you."

Nellie wasn't sure about the clan, or being

on the wrong side of the ocean, but she was becoming hooked on the hand-holding. The guy made her feel so good she didn't have to be bad just to get by. She also didn't want to think about whatever trouble she'd left behind, so she went with him into the dive.

Looking at the mossy stonework made her shiver with cold, as if there were a blizzard outside instead of rain. "You like living in this pile of rocks?"

"'Tis my home." He glanced down at her, and his pretty eyes darkened a little. "You've cheeks like new-bloomed roses."

Pleased by his poetic flattery, she bumped her shoulder against his. "You put them there, pal."

They emerged from a passage into a big room built of stone, with a tree growing up right in the middle to disappear into a ceiling of woven weeds and branches. What little furniture there was looked rough and crude, little more than logs and planks. Her skin started to crawl, and she skidded to a stop, jerking her fingers from his so hard the back of her hand hit the wall.

A huge horrible thing covered in muck

limped out of the shining, melting stone and trudged toward her, flashing big teeth as it let out a howl of rage.

"They shall suffer," the monster shouted.

Nellie screamed as it stretched out its arms. She ducked and ran past it…straight into the wall, which hadn't melted after all. She sapped herself and tottered back, her vision wavering. Through the pain she heard Edane call her name, but nothing was keeping her from dancing into blessed, empty darkness.

Chapter Two

NELLIE'S SHRIEK OF terror dumbfounded Edane, but her charge at the wall made him panic and lunge for her. Too late to stop her from colliding with the stone, he caught her as she fell back. Her eyes rolled up and she went limp in his arms.

"My lady?" He lifted her against his chest, and felt his gut clench as the scrape on her brow began to swell and bleed. Against his skin he felt the marks on her nape grow hot, and the muscles in his arm bunched as if in response. "Open your eyes. *Nellie.*"

She didn't stir.

Furious with himself, he stared at the wall,

but saw nothing. What could have frightened her so much that she'd tried to run away?

The sound of every member of the clan running into the great hall drew his attention. As they surrounded him, all of them tried to speak at once.

"By the Gods," Domnall said, setting down the timber he had balanced on his shoulder before joining Edane. From the wood chips caught in his light brown mane and scattered over his wet tunic he'd been working in the bathing chamber. "Did she escape the underworld?"

"Where found you this lass?" Mael demanded, as he appeared on the archer's left. The largest of the Mag Raith, and the clan's seneschal, he had greenery stains on his hands, and smelled of the herbs he'd been sorting in the kitchens.

"She's bleeding," Jenna said as she reached them. "What happened to her?" The chieftain's mate wore her hair short, but only because the overuse of her wraith power had nearly burned it off. "Did the maze grab her, too?"

Broden appeared across from Edane, his

stunning features harsh until he saw Nellie's face. Relief tinged with regret flickered over his features.

"'Tis no' my lady," he murmured to the falconer beside him.

"Then more still to come," Kiaran said. His kestrel, Dive, flew in to land on the falconer's shoulder, where she squawked so loudly she drowned out whatever he said in response.

"Please be quiet, all of you," Rosealise Dashlock said, and quickly applied the clean cloth in her hand to the lady's battered brow. The clan's housekeeper was always practical. "What can we do to help, Edane?"

"She needs warming while I tend to her injury." He glanced toward the kitchens. "Would you fetch my wound box, my lady?"

As Rosealise nodded and hurried away, Domnall took off his tartan and spread it over the fur before the fire. As Edane carried Nellie over and knelt beside him, the chieftain said, "I but jested about hunting lasses, Brother."

"'Twas another hunting her, Chieftain." As he lowered her limp body onto the plaid, he told Domnall of the demon he'd spied chasing the lady. "After I shot the Sluath, he flew back into the storm and vanished. I thought her a lad at first, until I drew closer. She sounds like you, Jenna, but she doesnae speak the same words. She calls herself Nellie Quinn."

He looked up to scan the faces of his clan, but no one appeared to recognize the name.

"Kiaran, Broden, patrol for the wounded demon," the chieftain ordered as he arranged the wet plaid over Nellie's torso to better cover her. "Mael, bring more wood to build up the fire. Jenna–"

"Dry blanket and bandages, got it." His wife gave the unconscious woman one more worried look before hurrying away.

Rosealise returned with the box of medicinal herbs and tinctures Edane kept in the pantry. She brushed back a tendril of curly blonde hair that had escaped her crown of braids before she took a bottle of whiskey from under her arm and uncorked it.

"Did the demon do this to her?" she murmured, as she handed it to him and frowned at Nellie's pale face.

"No," Edane replied. "When I brought her into the keepe she panicked. Mayhap she saw something that frightened her. She then ran into the wall." He nodded toward the spot as he used the spirit to clean the abrasion. "It fashes me. I didnae startle her, and before we came in, she seemed happy and at ease." He glanced at Domnall. "Although no' greatly impressed with our stronghold."

"Nor I when first we arrived." The chieftain eyed both of her arms and legs. "She's marked?"

"Aye. I found Sluath ink on the back of her neck." Edane reached under her short curls to indicate the spot, and felt another flash of heat along his arm. "'Tis but a wee band of it." That it didn't match his own skinwork made him wonder again if he was imagining the sensation.

Jenna returned with a soft wool coverlet and some of the old linens they used for bandaging. "She's pretty small, but Rosealise and I can alter one of my gowns for her to wear once she's awake," she told Edane. "You said she used strange words?"

"Many." He removed his wet tartan and covered Nellie with the fresh wool, tucking it in around her. "She first said to me, 'Thanks for drilling that goon. Thought for a minute there I was headed for the big sleep.'"

The chieftain's wife sighed. "Oh, yeah, she's one of my people." She studied Nellie again. "Not from my time, though, unless she's an actress in a period piece."

"She has such a short coiffure," the Englishwoman said, gently brushing back the short fringe of golden-brown hair on Nellie's brow. "It's as if she were attempting to pass as a boy."

"Believe it or not," Jenna said, "ladies are allowed to cut off their hair in the future. What else did she say, Edane?" Once he repeated a few more of Nellie's remarks, Jenna's face lit up. "You know, she might be from the roaring twenties. Girls in that era used a lot of slang, and wore their hair short. They were called flappers."

"Surely not," the housekeeper said, looking alarmed. "In my time that word meant a poor young girl trained and used for purposes of vice."

"Not on my side of the Atlantic. Our flappers were more like fun-loving rebels. The first wave of women's liberation, really." The chieftain's wife chuckled. "If she is from that era, then the Sluath grabbed her a hundred years before my time, and forty after yours, Rosealise. Getting to know The Great Gatsby here is going to be interesting."

Domnall frowned at her. "Didnae Nellie appear in your memories of the other ladies from the underworld?"

His wife thought for a moment, regarding the lass as she did. "No. I've never seen her before today, and why didn't she show up here, at Dun Chaill? According to my vision, this is where we were all supposed to go after the escape."

Edane saw the doubt growing in their expressions. "She's no' Sluath. She bleeds red, and the demon chased her as prey. He meant to claim her as a prize for their prince."

"Perhaps more slaves escaped by the sky bridge after we departed," Rosealise suggested. "We should expect she will regain some memories, as Jenna and I have, and then tell us what occurred."

"Aye," the chieftain said, looking thoughtful. "Yet until she does, Edane shall take charge of her."

The scent of something smoky and sweet tickled Nellie's nose, growing stronger as she rolled over. Being there felt as good as being wrapped in sun-warmed rose petals, but flowers didn't crackle. She opened one eye to see the gentle flickering of a fire across from her, framed by rough stone.

She didn't know why, but the golden-orange colors of the flames made her let out the breath she was holding.

Her arms trembled as she propped herself upright. A dull ache pounded just above her eyes. Under the blanket she was naked, but snug and dry. She didn't see any bruises or bleeding holes… Why would she think of that?

Cut it out. I'm alive, and that's all the matters.

She hadn't come to any swank joint, that was for sure. As Nellie glanced around the room everything appeared old, worn, or cobbled together. A half-burned candle provided the only light, but it showed her archer's bows of different sizes stacked in a corner. A quiver sewn of hide and bark hung from a peg hammered between the wall stones. The only other furnishings appeared to be a chest made of wood, a stool, and a small table that held the candle, a comb, and some coiled leather strips.

No hooch bottles.

Nellie felt relieved, although that seemed strange, too. She could sure use a drink right now, after…

In an instant everything came back to her. Falling naked into the pasture, being chased by the demon, Edane coming to her rescue, and then the ride on the flying horse. He'd brought her to his place.

Looking at the ancient walls made her remember the horrid thing that had come out at her. Goosebumps rose on her skin as she squeezed her eyes shut for a moment and tried not to shake. She'd tried to run from it, and then conked herself out. The monster hadn't been real.

She took in a deep breath, let it out, and opened her eyes.

No one else occupied the dismal room, so Edane must have put her here to sleep. She guessed from the Robin Hood gear that it belonged to him. She could smell that simmering honey scent of him all over the bed now, and almost felt him, too, as if he stood hidden somewhere in the shadows. That feeling of his unseen presence spread over her, and made her want to call out his name. She felt safe with him…but not here.

What if it's all fake?

She had a notion that she'd been someplace like this before now. From the way her stomach surged at the thought it hadn't been anywhere good.

Nellie eyed the door as she climbed out of the bed and wrapped the blanket around her bare body. Her headache grew instantly worse, but when she gingerly felt her brow, she found only a bad scrape over a small lump. That and a twinge of soreness in her neck seemed to be all she'd gotten from the conk. Then her fingers started to itch.

Touch something.

Grimacing, she tiptoed over to the bows. Reaching out, she took the one that looked the sturdiest. The highly-polished wood felt like glass under her shaking fingers. If nothing else she could clobber someone with it and–

The room went away and huge trees shot

up around Nellie. Ferns sprouted all around her feet, and patches of sunlight warmed her face and shoulders. The forest looked huge, and very old, but she felt certain that she'd never before seen the place.

You're a beauty.

She froze as she heard Edane's voice, and turned toward it. He stood a short distance from her, and chopped at a slender tree with a funny-looking hatchet. The sunlight blazed over his long scarlet hair, some of which he'd woven into thin, tight braids. He cut down the tree with just a few more strokes, then picked it up and balanced the wood across the back of his shoulders, curling his hands around the trunk on either side.

"What are you doing?" Nellie asked him. "Where are we?"

He didn't look at her or react to the sound of her voice. When she reached out to touch him, her hand passed through his arm as if it were just a moving picture.

Just like the monster.

He bent to pick up his ax and walked off. She followed him back to a rough-looking cottage with a thatched roof. He put down the wood, stripped to his waist and poured a bucket of water over his head. The tattoos on his arm made Nellie's throat tighten with fear. She'd seen those before, too, in the place that made her want to puke.

What if he's like that thing that was chasing me?

Four more men came, and with Edane they went inside the cottage. Nellie took her hand from the bow and started to follow them.

The forest vanished in the next moment, and she stood in Edane's room again.

Confused, Nellie stepped back from the bows. She sat down on the stool, bracing her hands against the table.

Edane appeared beside her, a blade flashing in his hand as he carved thin notches in the end of an arrow. His hair now hung much longer around his face. She watched as he set the knife aside and carefully inserted feathers in the shaft. A knock sounded, and a much bigger man looked in.

'Tis a storm approaching. The chieftain wants the boundary patrolled.

Edane nodded. *I'll ride out.*

Nellie jerked her hands away from the table, and the men vanished. She stared at her palms, and then at the table and the bow. Everything she touched made her see something that wasn't real.

She stood to back away from the table, making her forehead throb. Her hand shook as she gingerly touched the wound.

Ah, but you've been a very bad girl, haven't you? Something with copper eyes and claws gazed at her from the darkness in her head. *And a touch-reader. Born with your talent, too. That makes you worth taking.*

A streak of fresh pain blazed through her temple, and Nellie stumbled over to the bed and sat. For a long time, she held her head in her hands until most of the pain eased away. She glanced around the room, taking in every object.

I have to know.

It took all her nerve to rise again and go to the quiver, where she rested her hand against the laced hide.

Through that touch she watched Edane scraping and sewing the hide and bark together in another place. This time she kept her hand against it as she watched him and four other men with a bunch of people in robes who lived in a big forest. She learned that the people, who called themselves *dru-wids* and *Moss Dapple*, were not everyday plugs. A tall, shifty-looking *dru-wid*, who bossed everyone around, used Edane and the other men like guards for the tribe.

Galan Aedth. Just watching him made Nellie shudder. He was big trouble.

As she watched and listened to the men, she learned the names of the other four: *Domnall, Mael, Broden, and Kiaran.* They weren't happy working for Galan, but they never quit guarding the tribe. Edane sometimes bickered with Broden, the pretty boy of the bunch, but only because Broden ragged on him constantly.

Nellie wanted to sock the trapper right in the kisser for being such a jerk to her fella.

Domnall and Galan started having regular beefs, particularly when a big guy who looked like the *dru-wid* showed up with a curvy, dark-haired gal. Galan shot the lady with an arrow just before she and the big guy disappeared into a hole in the ground.

What a goon.

Nellie wondered if Edane knew just how

rotten Galan truly was. She could practically smell the stink of bad rolling off him.

Things got stranger when Domnall and his men found a dark-haired woman naked in an ash grove: *Jenna Cameron*. He and his guys treated her like a prisoner first, and then banded together to protect her against Galan. After an ugly brawl with the big *druwid* over Jenna, Edane and his pals left the tribe and the forest. On the journey, they were attacked by a horde of the winged demons.

Sluath.

Seeing the demons made Nellie's chest fill with jumpy rocks. Oh, yeah, she knew those guys. She couldn't remember from where, but they made her want to dig a hole and plant herself in it for good.

Edane and the Mag Raith had managed to dodge the demons, and then came to the dump they called Dun Chaill, where they decided to live. They'd had more troubles, and Jenna had been killed by a demon who threw lightning at her. Later she'd come back to life inside the castle.

Nellie sucked in a breath.

Maybe Jenna hadn't been dead at all. Maybe she's like the demons now.

Edane and the guys started rebuilding Dun Chaill. Later another woman with long pale curls and a fancy accent had fallen out of the sky into their garden. *Rosealise Dashlock.* Nellie held onto the quiver until she had seen all the crazy things that had happened to Rosealise and Mael, and how they had fallen in love.

The moving picture ended with Edane leaving to patrol the boundary. That must have been just a few hours ago, because he'd still been wearing the same old beat-up clothes when he'd found her.

That's been his life since he fell from the sky…like me.

Nellie's knees shook, and without thinking she braced a hand against the wall. She saw the monster again, only this time she could tell it was male. It didn't look like a human or a demon. The scars and distortion of his body and face made it clear that he'd been in some kind of terrible accident. The wall shrank to half its size as she watched him limp past her, his back bowed over the big rock he lugged.

He talked to himself in a language she didn't understand, and worked at building the wall until his hands grew bloody. He stopped only long enough to wrap his twisted fingers before he went back to work.

When Nellie had seen him build the entire room, she let her hand fall to her side.

She felt numb as she went back to the bed to huddle under the blanket. Her head throbbed, packed with all that she now knew about Edane and his clan and the monster that had built this dump. She blinked hard to keep from bawling, because she knew something else: the castle wasn't meant to be a home.

Dun Chaill had been built by the monster to kill.

So why were Edane and his clan living here? Didn't they realize how dangerous a place it was?

The door creaked open, making her instinctively close her eyes to feign sleep. Through her lashes she saw Edane slip inside with a tray tucked against his side. Over his shoulder he'd draped some kind of baggy dress. The scent of hot oatmeal and honey warmed her nose, but she waited until he came to the bed before she pretended to wake and looked up at him.

Nellie knew she couldn't get attached to him—at least not shacked up in this nightmare of a place—but still seeing him made her heart do the tango.

"Some of that for me?"

"'Tis all yours, my lady." He set the tray on the table and tossed the dress by her feet before he inspected her brow. "How's the head?"

"Like a pug in the tenth." She sat up, eyeing the food and wondering how she was going to get it past the fist-size lump in her throat. Then she saw his puzzled expression, one she'd seen before. *He can't understand me. Of course, he can't. He's not American.* "I mean it's sore, but I'll be all right. Say, I didn't mean to, ah, knock myself out like that. I got spooked by the place."

"You've endured much this day." Edane perched on the edge of the bed. "Forgive me for no' keeping you safe."

Nellie had to know one more thing. "You did swell." She touched his cheek, and kept her hand there until she was sure. "I'll try to talk plainer, see, so you can get my meaning."

"I'd be grateful," Edane said, his gorgeous eyes lighting up.

Giving him a little smile, Nellie thought quickly. She couldn't read him like the quiver or the bow or the walls, so that meant her touch would only read the past from things, not people. She removed her hand and tried to offer him a smile.

Sweet as Edane was, she couldn't stick around for the monster's flim-flam. Nellie couldn't remember what had dropped her in the middle of Scotland, but she knew she was in trouble here, so the what didn't matter.

She just had to get out of this place.

"There's much I must tell you," Edane said, and offered her a wooden cup filled with water. "'Twill seem mad, and impossible, but I vow to you, 'tis all truth."

"I'm all ears, honey bunny." Nellie took a sip and finally worked up a broad smile. "Hop to it."

Chapter Three

※

FROM THE EDGE of the remote highland village Danar watched the dissipating storm. Everything in him yearned to spread his concealed Sluath wings and soar up into the cold, wet clouds. It was how his kind moved through the mortal realm to cull human souls. He'd always relished the hunt, but here it no longer sustained him and his kind. Only in the underworld could they do as they wished with the humans they captured. Since becoming stranded in the mortal realm, he and his kind had to live as their prey did, hiding themselves in this plodding settlement.

Each day it grew more unbearable.

Two sentries trudged down from the

ridges, their harsh, low voices drawing the big demon's attention. Since being exiled, most of the Sluath bickered incessantly over the slightest disagreement.

"There's no sport in hunting the mud-crawlers in the caves," one said flatly. "The stone will not change, and they have no dark sight."

"So they could not have sealed the last gate," the second countered. "I told you, it was one of us."

Some of the *deamhanan* still believed a traitor among them had sealed off every gate to the underworld. It seemed a nonsensical notion to Danar, as the traitor would also suffer the deprivations of being banished to the realm of humans. No, whoever had done this had acted out of hatred. Since mortal magic had been employed to barricade the gates, it would seem like the work of the five Pritani rebels who had escaped them.

Yet since fleeing the underworld the Mag Raith had become immortal, like the Sluath. That had never happened in all the millennia since the demons had begun hunting and enslaving humans. Before the rebels, no one had ever escaped the underworld.

Danar paused.

That wasn't strictly true, but he had to cast his mind far back into the distant past.

"You seem troubled, *deamhan*," a low, gloating voice said. "Might I provide aid in some manner?"

Danar glanced at the overly proud face of the tall, dark-haired druid who had joined him. Galan Aedth had willingly agreed to serve the Sluath, which betrayed much of his dark character. In return for his help, Prince Iolar had agreed to resurrect his dead mortal wife. The bargain hadn't set well with the rest of the *deamhanan*, who despised mortals. The druid now had wings and some of the prince's power, however, and his ability to reincarnate made his mortal soul virtually worthless to the Sluath.

Galan had adapted well to being Iolar's mortal toady. This morning his gray eyes looked as chilly as ever, but the mortal betrayed his agitation by the dart of his gaze.

"You stink of failure, again," Danar said

mildly. "Lost more of your spies, have you? That won't endear you to the prince."

The druid's mouth thinned. "The few yet capable of searching shall soon die of plague. We must capture and transform more."

A shout from the guards made Danar turn to see a *deamhan* emerging from the fringe of the storm. His blackened, flailing wings barely kept him aloft. Danar snapped out orders to the guards to catch him. Despite their speed the injured scout fell to the ground, splattering the dirt with dark blood. Arrow shafts protruded from his withering torso, each emitting tell-tale wisps of smoke.

"He's been shot with iron," one of the guards muttered, backing away.

"I have eyes, you fool," Danar told him as he knelt down beside the dying Sluath. "Serca, who attacked you?"

"Pritani rebel." The demon writhed, clutching at the shaft sprouting from his neck. He tugged it out and choked out, "He took her. Your reader. She fell from… storm."

"You saw the Mag Raith capture Nellie Quinn?" Danar demanded. "Which direction did he fly?"

Serca uttered a strangled sound, and then went still. As all Sluath did in death, he turned ashen and his body began to wrinkle and shrink in on itself. Danar rose and backed away from the corpse, the taste of the iron smoke souring his mouth.

Galan cautiously approached to inspect the remains. "I ken those arrows. The Mag Raith shaman did this."

"Have this body burned," Danar told him before he headed for the biggest cottage in the Sluath-controlled village.

Inside the wattle-and-daub walls Prince Iolar had used their mortal slaves to greatly improve his temporary abode. Bleached hides and furs covered the floor, and the walls had been painted white. A huge brazier in the center of the front room blazed with white fire atop golden coals. Two young females, both recently captured, knelt on either side of a raised platform hewn from the palest stone in the highlands. The mortals, their hands clasped tightly behind them, stared up at the magnificent figure perched atop an enormous, feather-stuffed cushion.

"My prince." Danar bowed and waited to be addressed.

"Tell me you have reserved more females to entertain me," Iolar said, sounding bored as he studied his gilded claw tips. "For these two will not last the night."

Though the news brought by the dying scout might provoke the sullen prince's wrath, Danar knew that holding it back would only make Iolar more furious later, especially as the flapper had been locked away with a particular prize.

"Serca saw Nellie Quinn fall from the storm," he told the prince. "The rebel shaman, Edane, shot him with iron and took her. It would seem she did escape with the other females."

"Your touch-reader still breathes?" Iolar shot to his feet, his agitation sending a whirl of snow through the cottage. "What about my fucking treasure?"

"I've told you all. The scout died before I could learn anything more." Danar saw the fury growing in the prince's eyes and quickly added, "The reader knew much about our magic. She has seen us use the storm portal for centuries, and she knew what you valued. Sending your treasure to a time and place that only she knew would be shrewd of her. I believe that's the reason she came here rather than return to her era."

"So, I was right. All this time it was that thieving slut." Iolar grabbed one of the females by the hair and flung her across the cottage. She hit the wall, fell to the floor and whimpered. "Where is that idiot druid?"

"Here, my prince," Galan said. He had obviously followed Danar to eavesdrop, but now came in and bowed. "It seems the Mag Raith have ended another of your men. Mayhap we should create more spies to aid in our search for the rebels."

Danar held back a sigh as he stepped aside.

The prince kicked the brazier directly at the druid, showering him with its contents. Shimmering light engulfed Galan's form as the white-flaming coals bounced off and rolled away to turn into scorched stones. Since Iolar had given the druid some of his power as well as wings, Galan had learned to protect his fragile mortal body.

The power would not last forever, however. Danar looked forward to that day with ever-growing eagerness.

"I don't care about the rebels, you idiot," Iolar shouted. "The conniving bitch who stole my treasure has come here. Send your spies to find Nellie Quinn."

Chapter Four

※

EDANE STOOD WAITING outside the door of his chamber, wondering if he should insist on Nellie remaining in bed. On the chieftain's advice he'd told her everything they knew about the Sluath, and what little Domnall and Jenna had recalled about their escape from the underworld. All he held back was revealing their immortality and their powers, which the chieftain thought should wait until they knew more about the lass.

"I'm not in my time anymore, am I?" had been Nellie's only question. When he shook his head and told her she'd traveled back to the fourteenth century she seemed unsurprised. "Yeah, I figured. No cars or electric lights."

Coaxing her to eat had been difficult. Her limbs appeared too thin, and she trembled a great deal, suggesting the Sluath had starved her. Yet after only a few spoons of oatmeal she'd declared herself full, and ready to meet his clan. She'd also asked for several things that mystified him, and had pouted a little after he'd told her they had no mirror, rouge or lipstick.

"Guess I'll just have to look like an old lady for now." She held up the gown he'd brought, and pursed her lips. "Golly, and dress like one."

"You cannae help but be fetching," Edane said. "Even wrapped in wool."

"Looking good is job number one." For a moment she sounded uncertain, and then she squared her shoulders and fluttered her eyelashes at him. "Shoo and let a girl get dolled up, will you?"

Listening to the sounds of her dressing now made Edane smile a little. She might have looked the lad from her back, but the memory of seeing her naked at arm's length still made his blood run hot.

It had been too long since he'd felt the desire for a lover. Some unattached *dru-widesses* of the Moss Dapple had offered him sex now and then, but they'd reserved their affections for men of their own tribe. Knowing they were regarded as unsuitable as mates, Edane and his brothers rarely indulged in more than the briefest of trysts.

Now Edane couldn't help recalling the beauty of Nellie's high, small breasts, or speculating how perfectly they would fit against his palms. He'd never known a female with such a glowing bloom to her skin, as if she did nothing but laugh and smile. It matched perfectly the open bloom of her scent, like that of a glen speckled with wildflowers. The same warmth sheened her brown curls with gold, and glinted in the bronzed green of her eyes.

Yet for all her comeliness, Nellie's unique character tugged at him with equal intensity. She seemed very different than Jenna and Rosealise, and not simply because she appeared younger and spoke in such a strange manner. Edane liked her easy laughter, her airy movements, and the quick, lively way she spoke. Small as she was, she reminded him more of a bird. With her coloring she might have been a woodlark cheerily warbling to greet the dawn.

Mayhap one morning she'll wake in my arms.

The door behind him swing open, and Edane turned to see Nellie's bright smile. His gaze fell to the gown, from which she'd ripped away the sleeves and some of the length. She'd also dampened her hair and arranged it in curls over her ears and a straight fringe that covered most of the bandage on her brow. She'd put on the slippers he'd borrowed from Rosealise, but tied them in a curious fashion with strips from the gown, knotting the linen over her instep and tying the ends in a bow.

"Keep looking at me like that and I'll have to start signing autographs." She stood on her tiptoes to brush her lips against his, and her breath warmed his mouth. "Thanks for waiting."

The habit she made of kissing him unsettled Edane, but he assumed it was the custom of her time. He also enjoyed it too much to ask her to stop.

"I'm yours to command, my lady."

"Then you're every girl's dream fella." She stepped around him and took hold of his un-inked arm. "Come on, let's do the hello-theres."

Edane guessed she didn't like the Sluath skinwork on his other arm. Jenna and Rosealise had felt the same just after escaping the underworld. Yet each time Nellie touched him he felt the ink on his skin react to her. The same had happened to Domnall and Jenna, and Mael and Rosealise, yet their brands matched. Edane's looked nothing like Nellie's.

He wanted her to be his lady, but Jenna had no more memory of the lass than he did. Since their skinwork differed they'd likely never met in the underworld. Yet taking charge of Nellie meant he would constantly be with her until she adjusted to her new life at Dun Chaill. Perhaps in time she would come to see him as a desirable mate.

Certainly, the kisses she lavished on him gave Edane some hope.

He walked with her to the great hall,

where only Jenna and Domnall waited for them. Both looked welcoming, yet as they approached Nellie's hold on his arm tightened.

"You've naught to fear," he assured her before performing the introductions.

"Charmed, I'm sure." Nellie bobbed a little to Domnall, and then saw the direction of the other woman's gaze. "Say, sorry if I spoiled your rags, sister. Haven't worn sleeves since I was a tot, see?" She extended her hand. "Hope we'll be pals."

"Of course." Jenna smiled and clasped her hand for a moment. "We know you've been through a lot, and we want you to be comfortable here."

"Danny—Edane—said we're in Scotland. That's the place on top of England where they play bagpipes, right?" As Jenna nodded Nellie laughed. "Well, what do you know. I've never been west of…ouch." She touched her temple. "Jeepers, I just can't shake this hangover."

Edane heard a faint note of strain in her voice, and saw how her fingers trembled. "'Tis from a spell that compelled you to forget your past, my lady."

"Dinnae force a recollection," Domnall added, "for 'twill only cause you pain."

"Got enough of that from conking my head, Chief." Nellie jerked her chin toward the trestle table they used for meals. "You boys build that?"

"Aye." Edane guided her over and sat with her on one of the long benches. "When we came to the castle the hall stood empty. My brothers and I have since made all the furnishings."

Something flickered through her eyes before they rounded. "Huh. So, where's the rest of the clan?"

"Not far away," Jenna said, exchanging a wry look with her husband. "We didn't want to overwhelm you at first."

"Seven's hardly a crush," Nellie told her. "Now that I'm here, might as well let everyone have a good look at me."

Chapter Five

※

AS CHIEFTAIN, DOMNALL should have presided over Nellie's presentation to the clan, but he quietly handed off the task to Jenna. He could tell that his wife felt delighted to have another American at Dun Chaill, and wished to make the lass feel at ease. Standing back and watching Nellie speak to his men also gave Domnall the chance to observe reactions on both sides.

Although the American seemed to be as Edane had claimed, something about the lass did not suit her friendly behavior. Nellie's strange remark in the great hall—*Seven's hardly a crush*—also prodded his suspicions. She had known before meeting the rest of the clan how many of them lived at Dun Chaill.

Mayhap a fortunate guess.

Domnall didn't believe in luck, however.

In his role as the clan's seneschal Mael ranked second only to the chieftain, so Jenna first introduced him. As the largest of the Mag Raith he loomed over the little flapper, but Domnall noted again the ease in her expression. She seemed happy to meet his second, yet at the same time she drew back her feet, tensed and leaned forward, as if preparing to flee.

"'Tis a pleasure to have you with us, my lady." With care Mael took the hand Nellie offered and bowed over it.

"Aren't you just a man mountain?" She fluttered her eyelashes at him before smiling at his mate. "This gorgeous doll yours?"

Nothing in her voice indicated that Nellie felt nervous, but the chieftain saw a slight trembling of her skirt. Beneath it he'd wager her knees were shaking.

Mael grinned. "Aye, my wife and the clan's housekeeper, Rosealise Dashlock Mag Raith."

The flapper's hand remained steady as she

drew it back and regarded the other woman, perplexing Domnall.

What yet frightens her?

Rosealise offered a slightly cooler smile. Because her touch compelled others to do as she bid, she did not offer her hand. "How do you do, Miss Quinn?"

"Not too good with stone walls, Rosealise." She rolled her eyes up toward her bandage, and then made a comical face. "Sorry to be so familiar, but that's the ritziest name I ever heard, swear to gosh. Your mama must have known you'd be a dish."

Mael's wife murmured her thanks for the compliment and stepped to one side. Domnall noticed that she also began to watch Nellie closely. Since Rosealise had proven to be an excellent judge of character, he knew he could rely on her opinion if need be.

Jenna presented Broden next, who bowed politely but kept his distance. Domnall understood why. When Rosealise had come to them the trapper had mistaken her for a lover he'd known in the underworld, and had nearly come to blows with Mael over her. He'd not make that mistake again.

"Welcome to Dun Chaill, my lady," Broden said.

Nellie's eyes narrowed rather than widened at the sound of his rasping voice. Yet her gaze grew limpid again as she looked over his handsome face before meeting his dark gaze.

"Edane told me you're the clan's best fisherman." Her lips curved, and she gave him a pert wink. "I bet they see you and just jump out of the water to lay at your feet."

Her joke made Broden break into a rare smile. "No' quite, my lady."

That left Kiaran, the clan's falconer, who came to stand beside the trapper as Jenna introduced him. He didn't smile but inclined his head, making his red-gold hair blaze as it caught a shaft of sunlight. "Mistress Quinn."

Domnall couldn't fathom why Kiaran offered no words of welcome, for as ever his expression gave away none of his thoughts.

Nellie didn't seem to notice. "Hiya. What do you do for the clan?"

"Much." He nodded toward the other women. "Lady Jenna's our architect, and Lady

Rosealise cares for the household. What work ken you?"

"I'm always trying to look good and stay out of trouble, pal." She laughed as she held up her palms in a helpless gesture. "That's about it."

Dive, the kestrel perched on the falconer's strong shoulder, suddenly flared out her wings and uttered a high-pitched screech.

"Hey, pretty thing," the flapper cooed to the bird. As Kiaran stiffened, she said, "Bet you think I'm hinky for barging in on your family like this. Sorry about that. But I'm in a jam, and we girls got to stick together, don't we?"

The little raptor cocked her head and folded her wings again as she trilled a series of softer sounds that Domnall had never heard the kestrel make for anyone but her master.

"Quiet, Dive," Kiaran muttered, obviously annoyed.

Nellie's jaw tightened for a moment, and yet her lips curved as she said in a sweet tone, "She's lovely, and so well-trained. Maybe you could have her teach me how to fly."

"Likely no'. Excuse me. I must attend to

the green house." With that the falconer turned and retreated from the great hall.

Edane frowned. "I thought the work finished."

"The storm damaged the roof," Domnall told him, and used a hand signal at his side that only the men would notice. He then regarded his wife. "Perhaps you and the ladies should have a brew and talk in the kitchens while we see to repairs?"

"I've scones and a lavender tisane," Rosealise put in. "The strawberry preserves we just made should go nicely with them."

"I never met a cake that I didn't like." Nellie touched the archer's arm, giving him what appeared to be a reassuring caress. "Go on with the guys. I'll be fine."

Edane, Broden and Mael followed Domnall out of the hall, and found Kiaran waiting for them in the outer passages. The five continued out through the side entry into a cleared pasture where they had built a timber-framed structure according to his wife's specifications.

Loose wattle work and airy thatching allowed the passage of air and light. Inside, wooden benches held dozens of small clay pots containing herb and vegetable seedlings planted by Rosealise and Jenna, as well as sacks of crop grain they'd salvaged from the abandoned village of Wachvale. They'd all taken pains to make it appear that they used the green house for gardening work. During the building Edane had cast a spell that warded the structure within a permanent shroud of silence. This permitted the Mag Raith once inside its walls to speak freely without chance of being overheard.

Someone hidden within Dun Chaill had been watching them, and had nearly lured Rosealise to her death. In the months since she and Mael had escaped the underworld the Mag Raith had discreetly searched for the watcher. Although they found no sign of anyone living in the ruins, they continued to be on their guard.

"I shouldnae be long away from the lass," Edane said to Domnall before eyeing Kiaran. "Why couldnae you offer Nellie proper greeting before you interrogated her so?"

The falconer shrugged. "She didnae arrive

here as Mael's mate did. *You* brought her to Dun Chaill. We ken naught of her."

"I found her naked and chased by a demon," the archer pointed out, scowling now. "With Sluath ink on her. What more must you ken?"

"More than you desire, Brother." The falconer glanced up at the kestrels circling over the garden before he added, "She's mortal, and admits herself useless but for her beauty. What value can she offer the clan?"

"Little, just as a half-dead lad orphaned by raiders," Broden said, referring to how Kiaran had come to join their mortal tribe. "Or a bed slave's unwanted whelp. Yet you and I learned to be of use. By the Gods, Brother, she's only just arrived."

"I dinnae trust her," the falconer muttered.

"You trust no one, you cold-hearted arse," Edane said and turned to Domnall. "What say you, Chieftain? Will you offer the lass sanctuary, as you did Jenna and Rosealise?"

Nellie wore her happy, carefree manner like a mask over such fear and distrust that she'd shaken with it. Whatever she was hiding, Domnall knew it terrified her.

"The lass wouldnae likely survive long outside our spell boundary." Whatever Nellie concealed from them, he'd never permit her to come to harm. As for revealing his own misgivings, they would cause the disagreement between Edane and Kiaran to escalate into an ugly quarrel. "Mistress Quinn stays."

Chapter Six

❧

DEEP BENEATH DUN Chaill's stone floors, Cul woke to darkness and pain. For weeks he'd been imprisoned by rubble inside a corner of his underground sanctuary. His injuries, which at first had hampered his ability to dig through the debris, had gradually healed. Yet the sharp bite of failure still gnawed at him. The sudden cave-in of the passages around the tower had come without warning. In his arrogance he'd never considered that his beloved Dun Chaill might try to bury him alive.

Looking up through the blackness, Cul felt the burn of his anger sending new strength through his twisted limbs.

I will not die alone in the dark, even for you, my beauty.

Certainly, he could hold his unwelcome guests responsible for his present circumstances. After the collapse he'd heard Mael and Rosealise speaking above him. Doubtless their return from the underworld had triggered the catastrophe. Yet Cul had sent them there in the first place, so he had to share in the blame.

He'd also been fortunate. His iron warriors kept their watch at the spell barrier and the castle's warding spells were still intact. While they hadn't protected him from the cave-in, they had prevented his underground warren of tunnels from being accessed, as well as concealing the collapse. Without them his presence would have surely been detected by the Mag Raith as they had worked to repair the damaged tower.

Cul also felt a grudging but growing admiration for the hunters and their females. Despite all his efforts to drive out the Mag Raith clan, they had remained at the castle. Their determination to make it their home seemed gallant. Since they shared his hatred of the Sluath, he thought of them almost as allies.

Allies who would kill me the moment I approached them.

He rose from the mound of rags he slept on and hobbled to the end of the passage he'd slowly excavated. Stacks of broken stone and mounds of soil that he'd already removed lined the sides of the tunnel. If he added too much more, no space would remain for him to work. Still, he reached into the deepest part of the recess and dug.

Air whispered against his fingers.

Carefully, he grabbed the edge of a broken rock and tugged.

Earth and stone poured out of the hole, knocking him back, but it was followed by a steady stream of fresh air. He stood and dragged it into his lungs before he stooped to look inside. Through the narrow gap he could see the other side of the passage. Some rubble littered the floor, but otherwise it appeared intact. It seemed only the passages where he'd been trapped under the tower had been damaged.

A very welcome discovery indeed. He

would not have to leave Dun Chaill to hide in the ridge caves.

Bracing his hands on either side of the gap, Cul murmured a spell to hold back the looser debris, and then kicked out a larger hole. Hunching over, he squeezed his way through it. Limping down the tunnel, he checked each chamber he passed to find it intact. At last he reached the stores he concealed beneath the castle's kitchens, and retrieved a cask of wine and a smoked haunch of mutton.

His nature had made eating and drinking unnecessary for centuries, but he'd come to enjoy indulging in such habits.

The vibration of movement above him drew his attention from his meal, and he went to one of his observation posts. A series of mirrors that were angled to catch sunlight allowed him to spy on the Mag Raith during the day. He saw no sign of the hunters in the great hall, but heard through the listening tube the faint sound of female voices coming from the kitchens.

Too many.

Cul shifted position until he stood directly

beneath the voices, and listened. The other two women called the third *Nellie* and *Miss Quinn* as they spoke of their ongoing work at the castle. Nellie in turn laughed often but said nothing of substance. She seemed to be more interested in encouraging the other females to speak.

Curious now, he pressed his gnarled hands to the stone above him. Immediately he felt the newcomer's tremendous power. But as soon as he recognized her gift, he snatched his hands from the rock and backed away.

Somehow the Mag Raith had acquired a touch-reader.

Cul retreated down a long passage to his bathing chamber. He no longer considered Rosealise a threat to him. Since she had attained immortality the Sluath could not force her to use her persuasion power against him. Yet this new female was still mortal, and more dangerous than all the other intruders combined—especially if the Sluath had sent her to infiltrate Dun Chaill.

Whether they had or not, Nellie Quinn would have to die.

Chapter Seven

※❦※

WHILE SIPPING ROSEALISE'S flowery tea and nibbling on a currant scone, Nellie kept Edane's tartan tucked around her. Fabric made a lousy shield, but the scent of honeyed smoke he'd left on it made her feel protected. With its blazing hearth, shabby crockery, and abundant baskets of vegetables and fruits the big room they called the kitchens should have felt cozy. Instead the silent malevolence of memories permeating the old stone walls seemed to crawl all around her, waiting for her touch. She made sure to keep her hands in her lap while she listened to Jenna talk about her plans for Dun Chaill.

The other American adored the place

even more than the others, and thought she knew everything about it.

"The chance to rebuild a medieval castle is an architect's wet dream," Jenna said, her pansy-colored eyes as shiny as her dark, sleek bob. "We've got all the raw materials right here. Now if I could just find a master-level mason, and a herd of stone cutters, blacksmiths, carpenters, and, oh, a couple of tread-wheel cranes, I could make this place rival Guédelon."

Or hell, Nellie thought, nodding.

"Unhappily we're isolated here at Dun Chaill," Rosealise said, taking a sip of her brew. Pale curls had escaped her bun to softly frame her pretty face, but her gray eyes held a hint of steel in them. "Since there are no villages close to us, all of the work has to be done by the clan."

"You girls must stay busy."

Maybe not by choice, either. From what Edane had told her they thought this place was completely shielded from the demons. Maybe the monster had added a work-until-you-drop spell to the protective barrier. Or one that kept the clan from realizing the truth of Dun Chaill.

"We're up at dawn, every morning," Jenna said, exchanging a wry look with the housekeeper. "But our men work even harder than we do."

Nellie forced out a chuckle. "Well, that's why they come with all the muscle, ain't it?"

"You're very comfortable around the Mag Raith," Rosealise said. "I admire your fortitude and good cheer. The men made me feel rather nervous when first I came to Dun Chaill."

She couldn't admit that she'd learned about the entire clan from Edane's possessions. That was her ace card.

"They're nice guys, and they take care of their ladies. I can tell by looking at you two."

Keeping up the right number of smiles and laughs was wearing her out, but Nellie couldn't let down her guard for a second. The Englishwoman had said she'd been a governess in her time, but with her sharp eyes and shrewd observations she'd have made an excellent cop.

"Have you any inkling of what work you

did in your time, Miss Quinn?" Rosealise asked.

"Don't think I ever built anything except sand–" She grimaced as a throb of pain shot through her head. "Sandcastles at the beach. Jeepers, that hurts."

"Really, don't try to remember anything," Jenna said quickly. "Whatever spell the Sluath used on us still hasn't worn off."

"Yeah, well." Nellie shrugged. "What's past is past, right? Live for today, I say."

"Indeed, Miss Quinn, that we must," the housekeeper said as she added some honey to her mug before offering her the pot. "Have you anything you wish to ask about our situation?"

Why are you all so dense?

Nellie glanced at Jenna. "You said that you don't remember meeting me from the underworld. So, what was it like there? Were there, ah, joints like this one?"

Headache or not, hopefully that hint might jar a few memories for the chieftain's wife, who really needed to stop loving this awful heap of death.

"Not that I remember." Jenna described

the sky bridge she and the others had used to escape before she added, "If not for the Sluath I'd love to go back there and have a better look. The underworld seemed strange and unearthly, like the demons themselves. It's hard to believe such a spectacular place could belong to such evil beings."

"We've deduced that's how they're able to enslave the wounded souls they find so quickly," the housekeeper said. "In addition to our helplessness, we're too startled and bemused by their beautiful appearance to resist."

Not Nellie. When that demon had swooped down out of the clouds she'd run away. But she couldn't explain how she'd known he'd hurt her.

"These Sluath, they're all pretty angel types, like the one who came after me?"

"When they're alive, yes," Jenna said. "Domnall killed one who struck me with lightning. After death our men said that his beauty faded, as if it were just an illusion. His true appearance proved to be quite monstrous."

Yeah, I know all about monsters.

Wherever she had been before this place,

she'd been trapped and terrified. That feeling hadn't gone away.

That notion made the puzzle of Dun Chaill fit together at last for Nellie. The demons used magic and mind tricks to look beautiful to their slaves. They'd also made them forget their pasts and the underworld and whatever they'd done to them there.

Supposedly Jenna and Rosealise and the boys had escaped them, but where had they ended up? Right back at the mysterious castle where the Mag Raith had been taken by the demons. A castle filled with magical traps built by a hideous thing that didn't die and wanted to make people suffer—like the Sluath.

They never escaped, Nellie thought. *The Sluath built this death trap, and maybe used mind magic on them to make them think they did. Because of my touch I'm the only one who knows what it is.*

Telling them what she had discovered wasn't going to happen. She needed her ace card. Besides, they'd probably think she was crazy or, even worse, working for the demons. They might even lock her up, the way Domnall had Jenna when she'd first come to him. Or the demons might be listening in right now, and come for her, and make the rest of them forget she'd ever been there.

She might not remember her life, but she knew this in her bones: nobody put the squeeze on Nellie Quinn.

So she had to keep up this dizzy doll act until she could get out of here. She'd be happy to quit this place and escape the demons and their mind tricks. But she wished that she could take Edane with her. Leaving behind the handsome archer would hurt, but she couldn't risk him ratting her out to the clan, or alerting the demons to her escape. Even if she could persuade him to believe her, he'd never choose her over the guys. He regarded each of the Mag Raith as his brother.

Brother… Why did that word make her feel so blue?

"Are you feeling ill, Miss Quinn?" Rosealise asked. "You've grown quite pale."

"Just that headache." Nellie made a point to glance toward the narrow window next to the hearth. "Looks like the rain stopped. Jenna, want to go for a stroll with me? Fresh air would do me good, and I'd love to see what else you've done with the place."

Taking the tour would also give her a better look at the lay of the land. Once she packed up enough food and water to keep her going, she'd steal a horse and escape—this time, for real.

Chapter Eight

❧

WHEN HE HEARD low laughter coming from outside his new room Edane smiled and shouldered his tartan. The small storage room he now used for sleeping didn't offer enough room for a bed or pallet, but he didn't mind the cramped space. Nellie now occupied his bed chamber, and what sparse comforts he could offer he wanted her to have. Since she always slept in later than the rest of the clan, he waited for her to rise, so he could be the first to greet her.

For the three days that the lass had been at Dun Chaill she'd changed everything for him. He no longer felt the emptiness of eternity stretching out before him. Somehow he felt sure that Nellie would attain immortality, just as Jenna and Rosealise had, and she would need a mate. She'd already made it clear he was her favorite.

After rolling up his hammock bed, Edane stepped out just as the lass emerged from his room. "Fair morning, my lady."

Nellie grinned. "It is now, my guy."

Today she wore a dress he'd never before seen, which appeared to be parts of two other garments. The thin cream-colored wool skirt clung to her slim hips, where it had been sewed to the bottom of a chemise made of pale linen. She'd covered the seaming with a sash made of green and black plaid, which she'd tied in a bow at her side. She'd also made herself fingerless mitts from his tartan. One of his tunic laces encircled her head, and from that sprouted a cluster of gray and white ptarmigan feathers.

"What do you think?" Nellie asked, and twirled around, making the skirt flare. "I got some sewing stuff from Rosealise and put it together last night. Don't look too close at my stitches. They're awfully huge."

He made a show of inspecting her all over before he smiled. "'Tis an enchanting gown, my lady, but 'twill never look as lovely as you."

She laughed and flung herself into his arms, enveloping him in the wildflower scent of her skin. "You always make me feel like the prettiest girl at the party." As he moved to press her closer, she wriggled free and wagged a finger at him. "None of that, Mister."

"No touching?" Edane feigned alarm. "For us both, or only me?"

"You. For now. Later…we'll see." She seized his hand. "Come on, the sun's been up for at least an hour. Everyone's probably grousing that we're making them wait on breakfast again."

The rest of the clan had gathered in the great hall for the morning meal, but aside from a slight frown from the chieftain no one chastised them for their tardy appearance. Both Mael and Broden smiled as they took in her gown, while Rosealise's brows rose. Kiaran ignored them to feed a bit of bread to the kestrel perched on his gauntlet.

Jenna greeted them with a two-toned whistle. "What a great dress, Nellie."

"Thanks. Betcha it'll be all the rage in, what, five hundred years? Look out, Paris." She sat down beside the chieftain's wife, and eyed her mate. "Sorry we're late again, Chieftain. Takes me twice the time to look half as pretty as your girl."

"Indeed," Domnall said, eyeing his mate with a fond smile.

Nellie regarded Broden. "Then there's this guy." She rested her chin on her fist and made her brows go up and down in a comical fashion. "If you ever wake up bald, pal, it's because I shaved off your hair while you were sleeping to make me a swanky wig."

The trapper grunted, but pleasure warmed his gaze.

Nellie sipped her brew. "Mmm. This is delicious, Rosealise. Almost makes me wish coffee never gets invented. What's in this fabulous blend?"

"Lemon balm, cornflower and rosehip," the housekeeper said, her brisk voice softening. "With honey for sweetness."

"If she wasn't already your wife, big guy, I'd marry her," Nellie said to Mael, making the seneschal chuckle. She put down her mug.

"All right, I'll stop hogging the limelight. What's the clan got planned for today?"

Over the morning meal, the men discussed the day's work, which now included tending to the animals and thriving gardens as well as the ongoing renovations to the stronghold. Broden, who had taken charge of the livestock, reported on the black-faced sheep's over-abundance of wool.

"The villagers must have fled before the spring shearing, for their fleeces have grown heavy and become soiled," the trapper said. "Taking the wool now will keep them cooler for the rest of summer, and permit them time to grow enough fleece to weather the cold season."

"I've done some shearing," Mael said. "'Twill take two."

Rosealise nodded. "Jenna and I can wash the fleeces, and put them out to dry in the sun before we store them. I've never woven wool, but if we fashion what's needed to card and spin it, I can certainly knit winter tunics for everyone, and some proper mitts for you, Miss Quinn. Might I see one of those?"

Edane glanced at Nellie as she removed a

mitt and handed it to Rosealise. "Ken you how to weave, my lady?"

"Me?" She giggled and shook her head. "I barely know how to get out of bed in the morning."

"You're a very good dress maker," Jenna said as she passed her a platter of oatcakes. "In my time we buy nearly all our clothes ready-made."

"Still, someone had to make them, right?" The flapper surveyed the shabby tunic and trews she wore. "Maybe I could put together something for you, Jen."

"That's nice of you to offer, but Rosealise is actually teaching me how to sew." Jenna grinned at the housekeeper. "I'm all thumbs, but she's very patient."

Edane appreciated again how the chieftain's wife always managed to be considerate, even with a refusal. She truly wanted Nellie to feel at home with the clan. He cast a dour eye at the falconer, who now regarded Nellie as if she had issued a threat against Jenna.

"I can tell that you're great with birds." Nellie said to Kiaran, seemingly unaware of his ire. "It must be exciting to tame them and have them come to your hand like they do."

"'Tis work, Mistress Quinn," the falconer said, his tone chilly. "We all of us work here. Mayhap you've heard of such?"

Edane stiffened at the criticism.

"Sure. It's all you people seem to do," Nellie said, and slipped her bare hand in Edane's and squeezed his fingers. "I may not know how to build a castle, but I bet I can teach the clan how to have some fun."

Before Kiaran could reply Domnall said, "'Tis a grand notion. We've no' had a celebration since Mael and Rosealise returned to us." He looked at the falconer. "I need more nails and joists finished for the timber work. Fire the forge today."

Kiaran nodded but said nothing more, and quickly finished eating before he left the great hall.

"'Tis a fair morning, Edane," the chieftain said. "You should take Mistress Quinn out to the forest mound to fetch more workable iron for our brother."

Resentment flared inside him for a

moment, as Domnall's suggestion gloved an order to get along with his arse of a brother. Yet since the task would allow him to be alone with Nellie, he said, "Aye, if the lady wouldnae mind the trek."

"I love strolling in the woods," she said, and gave him a saucy wink.

Nellie offered to help Rosealise and Mael clear the table, but the housekeeper instead placed an empty willow basket in front of her.

"Would you mind collecting some wood sorrel on your walk?" Rosealise asked. "They make a lovely dressing for fish, but I've used up what little we had in the kitchen garden. They look like clover, but their flowers are different. Edane will point out the plants for you."

"Sure." Nellie took hold of the basket. "How pretty. Mael does nice work." She smiled brightly.

"Yes, he does. Oh, here." The housekeeper handed her mitt back to her. "How did you guess that he made it?"

"Saw him making one just the other day. Your guy seems very handy." She tucked the basket over her arm as she rose from the trestle bench and grinned at Edane. "Ready to go?"

※

Nellie felt the knot of dread in her chest loosen as she and Edane left the stronghold and walked through the lush grass. Outside the air smelled fresh and green, and felt just a little cool. Bright daylight spangled the dew that beaded everything, and cast gold coins of light on the trail leading into the trees.

So much better out here.

Now she just had to resist the urge to instantly run away, as fast and as far as she could. On the sly she had stolen everything she needed for her escape, and watched Broden saddle one of the horses. She felt sure she could do the same when it was time to scram. Leaving at night in the dark would be risky, but she figured it the best time to keep any demons that might be watching the place from seeing her go. She planned to make her break a few hours after Edane and the clan went to bed.

I just need something to keep them knocked out when I do.

At first making her dress had brought more, awful visions of the past. The fabrics had belonged to a man and woman who had been riding in a cart piled with fleeces. The monster had killed them and their horse, and burned the cart. But Nellie had also discovered that if she covered her hands with Edane's tartan, she didn't read anything from what she touched. Making two swatches of it into mitts gave her the first good night's sleep she'd had since arriving.

"Kiaran shouldnae speak to you with such little regard," the archer said as they entered the forest. "Pay him no heed."

"I don't." She realized how angry he was when she glanced up at his stern expression. "Hey, don't be mad at him. He just doesn't warm up fast to strangers. Besides that, he's your family, and there's nothing more important."

The hard line of his mouth softened. "You ever find something kind to say about everyone, even one who doesnae show you the same."

Lying to him made her feel lower than even Kiaran thought she was, and what she'd said about family made her head hurt again. "Maybe it'll rub off on him."

Strolling through the forest with the archer soon chased away Nellie's headache. As much as she hated the castle, the grounds around it were utterly enchanting. The huge old trees formed an endless emerald roof of leaves over them, diffusing the light into a dreamy softness. Flowering vines hung like streamers and garlands everywhere, adding festive splashes of color. Birds swooped all around them, chattering and singing like excited kids. The scent from all the growing things made her feel warm, happy and, oddly, safe.

Like Edane does.

"Wish I could live out here," she murmured as they stopped in a shady spot under an oak. "It's so beautiful and alive."

"Often I sleep under the stars." Edane bent down and plucked a heart-shaped leaf from one of the tiny golden blooms growing around the roots. He held it to her lips. "Taste."

She took a nibble, and the tart flavors of

lemon and apple made her snatch the rest from his fingers. "Jeepers, that's tasty."

"Wood sorrel," he said. "Clover tastes more sour and flowers in clusters of white or blush." He rubbed a fragment from her lips with his thumb. "Yet 'tis safe to eat as well."

Time seemed to slow as Nellie looked up into his eyes. She could see forever in them now, like an endless sky, like the kindness in him. Wanting throbbed deep and hot inside her. She'd bet he'd be the perfect lover for her, strong and tender, and yet just a little wild. Here Edane was all hers, as if the forest had become their private refuge, where they could be alone. No clan, no traps, no demons. Just a guy and a girl who wanted and lived for each other.

You're not that girl, and if you stay too long, you'll die with the rest of them.

"None of that, now." Nellie took a step back and knelt down by the herb patch. "We should bring back some of these little ones with roots, so Rosealise can replant them. Don't shake off too much soil."

He dropped down beside her. "You must have gardened in your time."

"I guess," she said, as that crazy scent of his swirled around her.

She focused on picking the wood sorrel. Falling for this guy would only keep her trapped here with him. That couldn't happen.

Once they had filled the basket, they returned to walk the trail. The shadows deepened around them as they approached a large mound of dirt that had been partially dug out.

"'Tis a hoard of travelers' belongings," Edane said. "Just after Rosealise came I opened it. It contains much clothing, weapons, tools, and such. We've been taking what we need from it for the stronghold and the clan."

That puzzled her. "Why would these people bury their stuff?"

"Domnall believes 'twas hidden by the attackers that killed them," Edane admitted reluctantly. "'Twas a common practice after a battle."

"How horrible." Even with her protective mitts Nellie didn't want to touch anything from the mound. "Do I have to carry the iron, too?"

"No, lass, I'll use the sled." He gestured to a wooden pull-cart by the mound.

Beyond it Nellie saw a break in the trees, and a pair of slopes between which ran a narrow trail. "What's over there?" she asked, pointing.

"'Tis the pass we rode through when first we came to Dun Chaill," Edane said. "I'd take you to view the glen beyond it, but 'tis a long ride over rough ground, and beyond the spell boundary that keeps us safe."

That sounded like the way out of this trap. "I thought you flew here on your magic horses."

"Only when there's a storm can we fly." Edane looked as if he wanted to tell her more, and then shook his head. "Under clear skies our mounts may only ride as any others."

"That's okay," she said, hating herself as she lied again. "I'd rather stay close to the castle than go exploring." Now that she knew which direction to ride, and that the horses would stick to the ground, she simply had to get out of the castle without anyone stopping her. "Say, do you think Rosealise would mind me making something for the clan after dinner tonight?"

"Of course, she wouldnae." He gave her a curious look. "What wish you to make?"

She wished she didn't have to do this. "It's a surprise."

Chapter Nine

❦

WITHOUT A STORM Galan couldn't use his Sluath wings, so he took a horse to ride out to the wide glen bordering the ridges. Danar claimed the scout had been attacked just south of Wachvale, the village where Galan's hired mercenaries were to have helped him raid and question the inhabitants. The men had instead slaughtered the villagers before becoming victims of the Sluath themselves.

Being reminded of that disaster didn't improve the druid's mood. Sending the few bespelled spies he had left to search for Nellie Quinn seemed to him utterly foolish. Like the Mag Raith, the wench could be anywhere now.

Relying on mortals had brought him no closer to the resurrection of his beloved Fiana. Neither had the Sluath and their empty promises.

As he passed by the ruins of Wachvale Galan reined in his mount to study the southern lands beyond it. Sheep no longer roamed the pastures, now overgrown. Doubtless other mortals had found and stolen the herd since he'd raided the village. He rode across the empty glen to the trees on the far side, but found no tracks or evidence left behind by the wench or Edane.

Fury rose inside his head, masking the world in a dull red. Danar had told him that the hunters could fly during a storm, which meant there would be no tracks. Once more the Mag Raith had triumphed over him.

The twisted shape of a long dead, lightning-struck oak caught Galan's eye, and silently blasted all thought of the hunters from his mind. Instead he imagined the split trunk whole, the gnarled branches heavy with leaves, and a tall, strong woman leaning against the rough bark.

Cannae be.

Swinging down from his horse, he hobbled the animal before striding over to inspect the dead oak. He reached out to the crumbling bark, noting that the weather had scoured away all but a small patch. Bits of shell, driven into the rough wood, still held it in place.

No one but he could have made out the symbol the shells formed: a crude tree with two twined branches.

"*Fiana.*"

Galan fell to his knees as the past engulfed him.

That day long ago had been overcast, and the wind hard and flinty. Still he had slipped away with his Pritani mate to escape the watchful eyes of his druid brothers. They still believed in the farce of their pact with the two tribes, which had established the breeding scheme to create a clan of indentured warriors. They'd even agreed to allow the largest and mightiest ovate among druid kind, to mate with their tallest, strongest female.

None of them suspected that Galan and Fiana found love together.

"Ye're mad," she'd said as she watched

him hammer the last shell fragments into the bark. "'Tis a sacred oak ye deface."

"I claim it ours," Galan corrected as he finished inlaying the glyph. "'Twill always carry the mark of our hearts." He turned to kiss her, and saw the tears on her cheeks. "Why do ye weep?"

"Ye ken we're no' meant to love." She pressed her hands to the bulging mound of her belly, caressing the unborn child she carried. "They chose us to bear a bairn to protect the tribes. 'Twas our sacred duty."

"So say the fools posing as the elders." He took her into his arms. "Come away with me. We can go to Britannia and make a home there. We'll raise the bairn ourselves."

"I gave my vow to the headman," she reminded him gently. "And ye to yer council. Our lad, he's too important to steal from them. The portents spell much grief and death if we dinnae breed the Skaraven."

"Then leave with me after the birth," Galan urged, and not for the first time. "They'll take the lad and be done with us. We'll escape and birth a dozen more."

"Say naught of leaving." Fiana pressed her

fingers to his mouth. "Ye're needed to train and keep watch over our Ruadri. The Gods wouldnae ever forgive ye for turning yer back on our son."

"I dinnae care." He took hold of her shoulders. "I want ye. 'Tis naught else in my heart. What matters a bairn they'll take from us the moment he draws breath? Let another train him."

"Ye're hurting me," Fiana said, and when he loosened his grip she sighed. "The elders foresaw Ruadri's coming." She touched her belly. "I felt the truth of their portents when he came to life in me. The Gods shall work through him to protect our tribes."

"Fack the Gods," Galan shouted.

"Husband, no." She grimaced, and glanced down. Dark streaks appeared on her skirts, and a small puddle appeared between her boots. "My womb's opened." She met his gaze and smiled sadly. "'Tis time to welcome our son to life."

Ruadri had been born the next morning, taking his first breath as Fiana bled out and took her last.

Now Galan turned his back on the shell

inlay and strode to his mount. His cursed son might be forever beyond his reach, but a Sluath spell was all that separated him from his beloved. He rode from the dead oak into the forest, following a path that no longer existed except in his mind. When he arrived at the site of the ancient druid settlement, which the Romans had burned centuries past, he jumped down and drew his sword.

Hacking through the brush, he cut a path into a grove of evergreen. Only a single stone marked the place, but when he brushed away the layers of soil and rot the faint lines of the twined-tree symbol appeared.

It was the grave marker carved by Bhaltair Flen, his old enemy. The meddler had known of his forbidden love for Fiana. He'd also seen to it that Ruadri had attained immortality as one of the Skaraven Clan.

Galan dropped his blade and bent over, grinding his brow against the cold stone. "I shall bring you back to me this night, my love."

Lifting the stone and tossing it aside, he began to dig.

Chapter Ten

⚜

AFTER THE EVENING meal Edane lit the torches in the great hall. Mael, Domnall and Kiaran had gone to perform the last patrol, but since Nellie had come to Dun Chaill there had been no sign of the Sluath. He suspected the chieftain and the seneschal had other reasons to leave the stronghold with the falconer, but refused to dwell on them. If Kiaran despised Nellie so much, he could go and live in the trees with his kestrels. The lass had done nothing to deserve his contempt.

As Edane finished his task he noticed Broden standing beside the hearth and plying a blade against a flare-ended rod. Small shavings flew from the rod into the flames.

"What do you there?"

"I make a chanter." The trapper blew off some dust before he showed him the instrument. "I carved many for the Moss Dapple's pipers."

"Aye, but we've none here to play it." As Broden put the reed end to his lips and produced a series of melodic notes Edane chuckled. "By the Gods. The *dru-wids* taught you that?"

The trapper lowered the pipe and shook his head. "I learned by watching them and practicing in secret." The rasp of his voice grew softer. "Your lass reminded me of how long 'tis been since last I made music."

That his brother had already paired them thus gave Edane much pleasure, but he could not claim her as such. "You ken I cannae yet call her mine. She's only just arrived, and she may yet favor another."

"Kiaran?" Broden uttered a rude sound. "'Tis only room in his heart for his screechers."

"Or you." As the trapper met his gaze Edane added, "Dinnae be daft, Brother. You've much to offer a mate." And in that moment, he hated him a little for his god-like looks and perfect mane.

"Naught will do for me but a lady with moonlit hair and skin soft as rose petals." Broden regarded the long pipe in his hands, his mouth curling as if he had amused himself. "If she comes to Dun Chaill, and if she wants me. Gods ken I'm no boon."

Edane felt a twinge of remorse over his own envy. Born to a headman's bedslave who died in childbirth, Broden had never had a chance to live among his own tribe. His sire had sent him as an infant to be fostered by the Mag Raith after his outraged mate had tried to strangle him. Although he grew to be a strong, wildly handsome warrior, the harm done to him in his cradle had forever ruined his voice.

Many females among the Mag Raith had admired Broden from afar, but the rumors whispered about his fostering had kept them away. The one Pritani lass who had confessed her love for the trapper had been scolded by Broden's father before the entire tribe. He'd also revealed his son's unfortunate origins, and assured her that the trapper would never have anything to offer a wife. The cruel scolding had devastated the lass, and ended any hope of Broden finding a Pritani mate among Edane's tribe.

"Your pale-haired lady shall come for you," Edane said to console the trapper. "Else why would the Gods send you dreams of her?"

"To torment me into madness?" Broden countered, but before Edane could reply he held up a hand. "I jest, Brother. I'm learning patience. Mayhap that's the reason for the dreaming."

A short time later the other men returned, and took their customary places around the hearth. Edane noticed that Kiaran had left his birds behind, which he did only when the kestrels patrolled the stronghold from the sky. The falconer's ability to see through the raptors' eyes allowed him to serve as sentinel. But why would the chieftain want Dun Chaill watched at night?

"Come and get it, boys." Nellie came out of the kitchens carrying a tray of steaming mugs. "I've made hot Hanky-Pankies for everyone."

Jenna and Rosealise followed her, and both ladies looked somewhat unsettled.

Edane went to take the drinks from her, which smelled not at all like the tisanes Rosealise usually made for their evenings. "'Tis a brew from your time?"

"Not really." She made a face. "You don't have any amaro, gin or sweet vermouth, see, so I had to make do. If you like it, I'll teach the girls my secret blend." She took one of the mugs, blew on it and held it to his lips. "Taste."

He cautiously sampled the drink, which tasted bitter-sweet beneath the heavy lacing of whiskey. Although drink no longer affected the Mag Raith since they had attained immortality, telling her so would only spoil her pleasure.

"'Tis very good."

"Pass them around, would you? I think everyone in this clan could use a little Hanky-Panky," Nellie told him, winking before she spied Broden's chanter. "Swell, that's just what we need. Say, if I hum something can you play the tune on your flute?"

Edane passed out the mugs, which everyone but Rosealise sampled.

"'Tis strong, but 'twillnae make you drunk," he said to Mael's wife. "Naught can now, you ken."

"Mael assured me of that, but after our experience in the vine trap, I'd rather abstain." The housekeeper frowned at Nellie, who was laughing with Broden, and then said in a lower voice, "Edane, I'm worried about Miss Quinn. She's not been entirely forthright with us. She lied about how she knew Mael made the basket."

Had Kiaran infected her with his suspicions? "Mayhap Nellie saw another at the work and mistook him for your mate."

"No, she was quite correct," Rosealise said. "Mael did weave it, but long before I came to Dun Chaill. Since that time, I've been making all the baskets we use, as my skills are slightly superior to my love's. Even you, dear sir, must admit that I cannot be mistaken for my husband."

So, the lass had not seen the seneschal at work. Edane couldn't fathom why she would lie about such a thing. "You believe she had some other purpose?"

"I can't imagine it, but yes. Her deception

troubles me." She glanced over at Nellie and Broden. "I have no wish to subject the young lady to new distress."

He understood what she meant. With but a touch Rosealise could persuade anyone to do as she bid. She could easily force a confession out of Nellie as to what, if anything, she might be hiding from them. Yet the housekeeper took great pains to use her persuasion ability only when absolutely necessary.

"I shall speak with her alone, later tonight," Edane said at last. "Nellie shall tell me the truth. She trusts me."

And perhaps it was time to trust her with the whole truth about the Mag Raith and their ladies.

꧁꧂

Nellie listened as Broden played back the tune she had hummed to him. He played the flute with ease, and she grinned as he hit every note.

"That's perfect, Brodie." When he arched his brows, she laughed. "You need a nickname, fella. Now, when we start to dance just play it a little faster, like this."

As she hummed the Charleston at the correct tempo, out of the corner of her eye she could see Edane and Rosealise quietly talking. No doubt that was about her. She'd said or done something to give herself away, and now they were suspicious. It made the fear worrying at her insides change from a blunt-toothed rat to an angry snake.

Got to make everyone want to guzzle their Mickey Finn. Get them moving.

"All right, we've got music." Nellie skipped over to Jenna. "Come on, sister. Let's clear the deck so we can show how Americans like to wear out their shoes."

The architect helped her move a few chairs away from the center of the hall, but once Nellie guided her into position, she looked worried. "I should tell you first that I never danced much in my time."

"Don't sweat it, Jen. The Charleston's a pushover," she assured her as she stood at her right side. "See me do this, and then just follow along." She performed the two step-and-taps of the dance forward and backward, and then watched Jenna's feet as she did the same. "Good, you've got it cold, first try. Now, when we do another set, shimmy your feet from side to side each time you step."

She practiced the four steps with the foot twists several more times before Jenna picked up the knack.

"Hey, this is easier than I thought," the other American said as she tucked her hair behind her ears and stared at her boots as she stepped and tapped. "So, when you dance with a partner, you mirror each other?"

"Exactly right. One more thing to add, and you'll have it." Nellie extended her hands palm-down, and swung her arms as she danced a full set. "Now you try that. Rosealise, come and join us."

"I daresay I should–" The housekeeper broke off with a laugh as Mael caught her by the waist and whirled her around. "Waltz with my husband instead."

"Give a try with me, love," the seneschal urged, and demonstrated the steps with surprising expertise. "'Twill make your skirts flutter quite fetchingly."

"Oh, very well." With obvious restraint

Rosealise went through the steps, and then chuckled. "For such a simple dance it is very charming."

"Attagirl. We'll make a floor flusher out of you yet." Nellie nodded at Broden. "Heat us up now, Brodie?"

The trapper began to play, and Jenna danced alongside Nellie while Mael and his wife watched and followed them both. Aside from a few missteps everyone caught on, and soon were hoofing it as if they went to the club every night.

The club.

Nellie saw the hall waver, and the ghostly image of another place appeared over it. The joint looked dark and crowded, and she could smell the stink of hooch and sweat. A group of perspiring musicians stood on a small stage playing behind a frantic mass of dancers. Everyone was doing the Charleston except Nellie, who stood at the back with a drink cradled in her hand, and her fingers running up and down a long strand of–

Say. A tall, cadaverous-looking man walked slowly past her. As he did his big yellowed teeth flashed. *Looking swank tonight, Baby.*

In an instant the man and the club vanished, leaving Nellie with a pounding head and a throat sandpapered by fear. She glanced around at the others, and saw that Domnall and Kiaran had come closer to watch the dancing, but no one was looking at her except the falconer. Coaxing the chieftain to dance would be tough, she thought, but Kiaran's disapproving expression made it clear he'd rather jump in a loch. On the bright side, he had picked up one of the mugs and was drinking it down.

"Come on, my man," Jenna said as she seized her husband's hands. "Don't look so worried, I'll show you how."

Nellie turned to find Edane just behind her, and nearly screamed. *Pull yourself together, doll.* She held out her arms. "You can't let the chieftain show you up now, right?"

The archer nodded, and took hold of her forearms as he fell into step with her. He danced with the natural ease of experience, and added a spin that lifted Nellie off her feet to whirl around him.

"You've danced before this," she teased him.

"Aye." Unhappiness flickered over his face before he spun her again. "So have you."

Nellie laughed despite the fact that her heart ached. "I was born for it, pal." This was both their first and last dance. After tonight she'd never come back here, and never see him again. "Say, feel like sneaking away with me a little later? I want to show you something." She stroked her fingers against the hard muscles in his unmarked arm. "Something you'll like, I promise."

"'Tis naught you could do that I'd despise," Edane told her, and moved in an extra step to say against her ear, "Naught, my *peyrl*."

The word he called her made a funny sound rush in Nellie's ears. Without thinking she reached for her throat, missed a step and nearly tripped over her own feet.

"Hey, you're distracting me, you bad boy."

By the time Broden finished the song all the men but Kiaran had learned the steps, and the clan laughed and clapped as the trapper bowed to them.

"'Tis an invigorating rollick," Mael said, and drained his mug with a few swallows before beaming at his wife. "But my lady, she's the swan."

"Ever the flatterer, my love." Rosealise kissed his cheek before she smiled at Nellie. "Thank you for teaching us the steps, Miss Quinn."

"Next time I'll have to show you the foxtrot. A bit like a waltz, but faster." She saw the falconer glowering at her again. From the unsteadiness of his hands at his sides, Kiaran was already in deep with Mickey Finn. "I've got more Hanky-Panky staying warm by the fire, too, if anyone's still thirsty. Edane and I are going for a little stroll."

She tugged the archer along with her and hurried out of the hall.

※

Edane went along with Nellie until they entered the outer passage, where he drew her to a stop. "Mayhap we should first talk, my lady."

"I only said that so I could get you alone." She took hold of his hands and began walking backward. "I've got one more surprise from my time, but this one is just for you."

Her excitement seemed genuine, and Edane didn't wish to spoil her fun. "'Tis another dance?" he asked as he followed her down the passage.

"You could put it that way." She stopped in front of her chamber and went behind him, reaching up to put her hands over his eyes. "Now, open the door and step inside."

He smelled melted beeswax and heather as he crossed the threshold, and felt the warmth of the fire from the hearth. "What now?"

"Keep your eyes closed." She took her hands away. "Don't look, or you'll spoil it."

"It?" He heard her dress rustle. "Nellie—"

"Not yet." The bed's ticking crackled, and then she uttered a husky sound. "Okay. Now you can have a gander."

The sight of her reclined on the thick white furs sent hot blood rushing to his head. That she lay before him so wantonly didn't startle him as much as the garment she had donned. It might have once been a shift, but she had cut away the sleeves and much of the bodice. He could see the curves of her breasts, and the subtle shadows of her nipples. She shifted her legs, which now showed thanks to the skirt's slit sides, and rubbed one foot along the other shin in a sensual manner.

"Welcome to our petting party," she said, extending her arm. "Come here and I'll show you how it goes."

Edane wanted nothing more than to obey her command, but he'd first be sure what she offered, and why. "You wish me to bed you?"

"I'd like you on the bed." When he didn't move, she patted the ticking. "You don't have to do anything, fella. Just get close to me, and let's see what happens."

Sensing an oddness in her tone, he sat down beside her. "You dinnae ken what comes from inviting a man to your bed, my *peyrl*?"

"Oh, yeah. Making whoopee." She stroked her hand over his forearm, her touch light as silk. "Sorry. I mean, I know what sex is. What if we just get to know each other a little better first? A little kissing, a little petting, then we can decide if we want more." Her eyelashes fluttered. "Unless you had too much Hanky-Panky already."

Pulling off his tunic and stretching out

beside her felt like a mistake. He was a man, not an iron warrior. But Edane decided his self-control strong enough to see how far she would go. In truth he welcomed the chance to return her kisses and caresses, but until he understood why she offered herself now, he would not take her.

As Nellie rolled toward him, he propped his head on one hand and used the other to bring her fingers to his mouth. Watching her eyes, he realized she was expecting him to put his hands on her, as if that were part of a plan.

'Tis no' about desire for her, Edane thought as he kissed each fingertip before pressing her palm to his bare chest. "Pet me as you wish."

Nellie uttered a short laugh, her hand trembling against his flesh. "Don't tell me you're too shy for this. I know you want me."

"Aye." His blood ran hot as he curled an arm around her waist and pulled her closer. "I've imagined it every night since you came, my lady. Ever you fill my thoughts with your bright beauty. The morning song of your voice becomes the music of my dreams. The secrets in your eyes, a glen waiting for me to find my way to you."

"Don't say things like that." She closed her eyes, gripping his shoulder as she pressed her face to his neck. "I'm just a gal looking for a good time."

Edane tipped up her chin, and brushed a soft kiss over her tight lips. When she finally looked at him, he saw tears brimming. Was she afraid of him now?

"You're safe with me, lass. Always and ever, I swear to you."

"I don't want always." She put her hands in his hair, curling her fingers through the heavy strands. "I want tonight."

Her mouth came to his, cool and damp, and he tasted the tear that spilled from her cheek to seep between them. The sound she made as she opened her lips held the desperation of a sob, followed by a moan so deep she shook with it.

Kissing her began as a comforting, a prelude to more soft words and coaxing her to entrust him with her secrets. But Edane felt his intention fade as she responded with needy hunger, her body pressing to his. She felt so lush and alive he wanted to rip apart the thin fabric separating her breasts from his chest. He needed her skin on him, her hands, her lips. In another moment she'd drive him to madness, and he'd forget everything but her. He took hold of her nape to tug her away, and felt her skinwork burn against his fingers.

Edane jerked back as his marked arm lit up with amber fire.

Chapter Eleven

✦

DARKNESS SWALLOWED EDANE, only to be sluiced away by ribbons of blue-white light. Blinded for a moment, he blinked, and then saw the two figures that had walked out of the cascade of light. The towering Sluath loomed over the small woman at his side, his wings glittering with dozens of honed blades. The female, dressed like a goddess in a pale green gown, looked at him with a faint smirk, and worried eyes.

Hold your tongue until she's close.

Aye, and he would, but he hated the sight of her with Danar.

"You've made use of the Pritani?" the Sluath said as he stopped to inspect Edane where he hung by his chains from the punishment pillar.

"Did you think I wouldn't?" Nellie sauntered over to stand before him, lifting her skirts to avoid the spatters of blood he'd dripped on the white stone floor. "I think he's starting to like being my bed slave." She let her hand drift down his chest to cup the front of his trews, where his shaft instantly swelled heavy and hot. "All it takes is a touch now, and he's ready for me."

"Turn me loose and I'll skewer ye proper," he snarled in her face, pouring all the fury he could into the threat.

"Still a little mouthy, though." She slapped him, hard enough to make his head snap to the side. "We're working on that." She kissed the reddening mark on his cheek, her lips cool against the sting. "If he wants to eat, he has to talk sweet to me. Say something nice, boy, or no supper for you."

Edane remained silent, glaring past her at Danar. He hated the demon above all the others, especially when the hulking Sluath came to inspect him.

"Insolent for such a weakling." The demon

approached him, and clouted him so hard his head seemed to explode.

Nellie watched without expression as Edane's knees buckled, and his body dropped as far as the chains would allow. As pain throbbed through his face fresh blood dripped from his nose to add new stains to the floor.

"Oh, well, more for me," she said cheerfully as she went over to a table heavily-laden with food, and scooped up a handful of berries. "Get anything for you, Boss?" she asked as she nibbled. "I've got that wine you like, the one made with that French girl's tears or something."

The big demon eyed Edane before he shook his head. "Enjoy yourself while you can. Once we return from the next cull, it will be your time, and this one will go to the arena to decorate a blade."

"Aw, I don't get to keep him?" Nellie pouted. "After all this bed training, too. What a waste."

Danar chuckled. "It's what he wants, more than you, little reader." He trudged over to the wall and disappeared through another shower of white-blue light.

The berries scattered on the floor as Nellie rushed over to Edane.

"Have you lost your marbles? I told you not to look at Danar like that," she said in a low, shaking voice as she released his manacles. "What if he'd hit you in the chest?"

He fell to his knees, holding her against him as sharp needles of sensation latticed through his numb arms, and relief flooded his heart. "Then I'd no' be going to the arena, Mistress."

She dragged him to his feet and tottered as she helped him to one of the softly padded chairs. There she pushed him down and used her sleeve to staunch his bloody nose while she muttered under her breath.

"Lass," he warned. Although the demons rarely watched them, the risk she took was too great.

"I don't care." She knelt before him, and put her head in his lap. "They leave for the cull tomorrow, Danny," she said, murmuring the words against his thigh. "They'll lock me away with all the treasures before they go."

Edane caressed her shining curls. "Aye, just as ye reckoned." When she looked up at him, he stroked his thumb across the soft curve of her lower lip. "We've tonight, then."

"Yes. All night." Nellie delicately pressed her mouth to the bulge of his stiff cock before she smiled up at him. "Come to bed now."

※

Opening her eyes to see Edane staring at her made Nellie flinch. She twisted out of his arms, scrambling to get off the bed, and backed away from him.

"What did you do to me?" she demanded. "How did you make me... What was that place? Why were you chained up?"

"Naught of my doing, my lady." He stood and reached out to her. "You saw me in chains? Beaten by the large demon called Danar?" When she nodded, he sat back down on the bed. "'Twas a memory of the underworld where, 'twould seem, I served as your slave."

For an instant Nellie thought she'd be sick. "No. I'd never... I couldn't."

"'Twas some manner of scheme, then, to deceive the Sluath." Edane touched his marked arm. "'Tis no' that your skinwork differs from mine. I'm no' marked as a slave." He shook his head, a strange bitterness flattening his mouth. "They chose me as a sacrifice."

She stared at him. How could he be so calm about it?

"You were in chains. I called you my slave. I said all those horrible things. I did nothing to stop that demon from hurting you."

"'Twas a ruse, I'm certain. You were different after he left the chamber." His gaze locked with hers. "I reckon there we became lovers, my lady."

Nellie didn't know what to say to him. "Why don't I remember you, then?"

"They took memory of me from you." He sounded almost glad about that. "'Tis late, and you should rest." He went to the door. "On the morrow we must speak with my clan about this. Fair night, my lady."

Edane left and Nellie couldn't blame him for wanting to get away from her. She'd done nothing to protect him in the underworld. Whatever he'd felt for her before the vision had been rubbed out.

It's for the best. He'll hate me anyway after I scram.

She went to her wash basin and splashed her fiery face with cold water. The shame she felt wasn't the only thing torching her insides. She'd wanted him so much her body had practically steamed. It still did, and it tempted her to stay and come clean to him and the clan. Maybe they'd give her another chance if she told them everything she knew, and found a way to get them out of this prison.

Are you loony? They'll never believe you, especially after Edane tells them what you did to him. They'll know you're a fake and a cheat. The way Kiaran hates you, he might even kill you for it.

Pain hammered away the voice as Nellie bent and dragged out the satchel and fleeces she'd squirreled away under her bed. The food and waterskins she'd packed made the traveling bag bulge. She had to comb out the fleeces with her fingers before she put them on the ticking and covered them with a blanket. Molding them into shape took some time, but at last she had something that looked like her body huddled beneath the wool. Hopefully it fooled Edane long enough for her to put some distance between her and Dun Chaill.

Pulling the shift over her head, Nellie dropped it to the floor. From beneath the ticking she took out a dark blue linen gown and brown wool cloak she'd filched from the laundry before Rosealise had begun the day's washing. Because Jenna had been so kind to her, stealing her clothing seemed particularly cruel, but they were almost the same height, and the Mag Raith all had sharp eyes.

"Sorry, Jen." She held up the soiled gown to her front. "I just need to be you until I reach the pass."

Chapter Twelve

※

RIDING BACK THROUGH the night to the Sluath-occupied village gave Galan ample time to rethink his intentions. Even with the power Iolar had given him he could not hope to prevail over the demons, unless he resorted to using iron weapons and taking them by surprise. Although his anger had swelled beyond even his greed for immortality, he'd never be able to kill them all. Then Iolar would take pleasure in making him suffer horrors unimaginable before he choked or burned or beat the last breath from him.

"He needs me too much to end me, Fiana." The dread he'd once felt over the prospect of dying as a mortal had vanished when he'd found her grave. Perhaps he'd gone a little mad, but he had been parted from her too long. He'd have her alive and breathing in his arms, this very night, or embrace oblivion without her. "But I'll risk it, aye, and he'll give you back to me."

A cold ache spread down his back from the bag strapped over his wings. He had carried the memory of Fiana too long to be plagued by the weight of her bones, but the chill of them spread through him, making his hands stiff and his legs numb.

At the entry to the village Galan reined in his horse and dismounted, stumbling and scattering grave dirt around him from his filthy garments. He leaned against the animal's side for a moment until his legs steadied, and noticed the white froth streaking its hide. White breath bellowed from the exhausted mount's nose, wafting into his face.

Had he ridden here without stopping to water the nag? He couldn't remember.

Unsteadily Galan made his way to the center of the village. The guards who moved to stop him from entering their prince's abode took a hard look at his face in the torchlight, and then stepped aside.

"We're no' to be disturbed," Galan said to them, entering the cottage and kicking the door shut behind him.

Braziers surrounded Iolar, who lay immersed in a huge tub of steaming, flower-scented water. He didn't open his eyes but sniffed before he said, "You stink of the grave, Aedth."

"And you of posies, my prince." Galan looked at the pair of quivering mortal females attending the prince. "Get out."

The prince sighed as the wenches fled the cottage, and sat up to regard him with exaggerated patience. "I see you did not bring Nellie Quinn to me. Do you think it wise to present your liege with nothing but your uselessness? Again?"

"I went in search of the wench, but found my wife." He pulled the bag from his shoulders and cradled Fiana's bones in his arms, rigid with the wrath of centuries. "You shall resurrect her for me, as agreed."

Iolar studied his face as he rose from the

bath and wrapped himself in a long white fur. "I had expected this, but not this soon."

Galan peered at him. "'Tis what you vowed to give me."

"I don't mean your lost love," the prince said, sifting through his wet locks with his claws. "You've lost your mortal fear."

"I lost everything the day Fiana died." He looked down at the dirt-crusted bag. "Every lifetime since then I've sought the means to reclaim her, that I might once more live as a man. 'Tis all I've desired, this one boon." He met the prince's curiously calm gaze. "Aye, and I've done all you've demanded of me. I've abandoned the Gods and druid kind. I've brought you to sanctuary and turned helpless mortals to your aims. I've killed for you. You shall do this for me now."

That he shouted the last words didn't seem to offend Iolar, who even smiled a little as he poured wine into a goblet, and brought it to Galan. "I cannot bring her back, Aedth. The fact is, I do not have the power to resurrect the dead."

The bag dropped from his hands as he stared at the prince. "You *lied* to me?"

"I agreed to foolishness spouted by a proud, ridiculous druid who dared to bargain with the Prince of the Sluath." He pushed the goblet into Galan's grimy hands. "I tell you the truth now because you're no longer that fool."

A soft roaring in his ears made it difficult to understand what Iolar was saying. "I'm no'?"

"Perhaps you should recall what I've already given you." The prince tapped a claw against the center of his chest. "You endured the wings I built on your back so you could fly with the storms. You took my own power into your body to restore your magic. Each day since, you have lost a little more of your... foolishness. You've grown to understand the *deamhanan* and our ways. Soon you will awaken to what you were truly meant to be, Aedth. As for this obsession you have with your mortal mate..." He glanced down. "She's lost to you."

"You cull souls. I've watched you tear them from the bodies of mortals." Galan stared down at Fiana's remains. "How can you no' return them, and bring them back to life?"

"We can take souls only from the living, in

the final moments before they die. Once the life of the body ends, mortal souls go beyond our reach." Iolar walked up to the pale stone platform to recline on his feather-stuffed cushions. "Only one known to us possessed the power of resurrection, and that was long before you were first spawned."

Galan managed not to shout, but only just. "Who?"

"A Sluath halfling sired on a slave by my father when he ruled the underworld. During his rule we sometimes bred our own kind in that fashion. Something to do with the bastard's Pritani blood allowed him to revive the dead, or so the ancients claimed." He yawned. "He could not live as Sluath or mortal, and he went mad. That is why when I took the throne, I put an end to breeding with slaves. My half-brother fled to the mortal realm before I could kill him, and there died as miserably as he existed."

Befuddled and blank of thought, Galan drained the goblet of wine, and then dropped it to the floor as he picked up the bag of bones. "I'll leave you now."

"Aedth, understand that I allowed you this

little confrontation as my gift to you," Iolar told him, his voice velvety with menace. "If you ever speak to me again as you have tonight, I'll nail you to the floor and allow Meirneal to feast slowly on you. Starting with your cock."

The threat did not terrify him. Like everything the prince had said it was a truth that no longer interested him. Galan left the cottage and walked back to where he had left his mount. He would ride into the ridges, and find a protected nook where he might rebury his beloved. There he would put blade to veins, and seal her new grave with his own blood.

A hulking shadow intercepted him halfway there. "You nearly killed that horse, you idiot."

He looked up into Danar's copper eyes. "Apologies. I brought my wife's remains back. Iolar told me that mortals slaughtered the only Sluath who could resurrect her, so I'm done with you. Keep your facking horse."

The big demon's expression shifted from anger to bafflement. "Our prince never speaks of his half-brother. He's slaughtered demons for reminding him that he once existed."

"'Twould seem his ire has faded," Galan said dully. "Mayhap he mourns him now."

"If he died." Danar's voice dropped lower. "Before he escaped the underworld Iolar badly wounded the halfling. He's never been seen or sensed by any of us. But we never found his body, or proof of his slaughter. To keep the peace, we told Prince Iolar he was dead."

"Was the halfling immortal?" As Danar nodded, the roaring faded from Galan's ears. "Tell me more of him."

Chapter Thirteen

※

SINCE NELLIE QUINN had arrived Kiaran had begun spending the first half of the night in the newly-rebuilt tower. From there he could easily watch for movement in most of the roofless passages as well as remain connected to the eyes of his patrolling kestrels. Tonight, Dive and her mate had taken wing to glide and hover over the stronghold, their small heads still as they scanned below them with their keen vision. Like all their kind they preferred to work during the day, but they could hunt in twilight and moonlight to provide food for fledglings during nesting season.

The chieftain had ordered him to have his kestrels patrol the skies after dark for the

Sluath, but Kiaran had commanded them to also watch for Nellie Quinn.

Making plain his distaste for the brazen little wench had not swayed the clan against her, but Kiaran felt sure she would soon betray herself. She certainly gave herself away to him every time she opened her lying mouth. Her carefree, laughing façade concealed a selfish, calculated nature, one that she took great pains to conceal.

He'd argued at length with Domnall about allowing Nellie to remain at Dun Chaill, especially as they knew so little of her. The chieftain had remained unswayed.

"Why shouldnae we offer shelter to her?" Domnall asked. "Whatever her past, 'tis plain she hasnae anyone to protect her. I'd reckon you'd fathom her plight better than any of us."

Kiaran did understand, but not for the reasons his chieftain assumed. He had recognized what Nellie Quinn truly was from the first time he'd watched her artful pretense. She wanted the clan to believe her frivolous, shallow and unskilled. She had charmed them all to believe her clever lies. Even Edane, who usually had more sense about others, had been wholly taken in by her. Only Kiaran had picked up on the signs of her deception, and the depth of it.

One dark heart cannae remain masked from another.

Many times since awakening in the ash grove Kiaran wished he had told his brothers the truth about his boyhood, and the massacre of his tribe. Yet that would mean admitting what he had done on the day of their final hunt. Although he'd spent his immortal lifetime trying to make up for it, it had been his final betrayal that had damned them all.

In the tower niche Kiaran braced his back against the mortared stones and closed his eyes to reach out to the patrolling kestrels. Seeing Dun Chaill from the air through his connection with his raptors also gave him a sense of how far the restoration had progressed. By winter the clan had to ready the stronghold to withstand the highland's harsh winds and heavy snows, and provide adequate shelter for the stock to keep them alive through the cold season. Much remained to be done.

This foolishness with the American wench had them all distracted from their work. Was that part of her aim? Even now were the Sluath preparing to attack Dun Chaill?

Dive caught a flicker of movement near a gap in the curtain wall, and descended to perch on a birch branch. Although she didn't think in words as Kiaran did, he felt her wings shift and her talons ease, as they did in the presence of a clan female. That would suggest she saw either Jenna or Rosealise, but neither lady would have gone out alone in the night.

Domnall's last warning echoed in his head. *Assume naught about the lass until you've proof.*

Kiaran used his power to peer through the bird's eyes, and made out a slight figure concealed by a dark hooded cloak. The kestrel had a limited sense of smell, but could see colors beyond Kiaran's own vision. He knew that, to the raptor, Jenna's power showed through her garments in a pale violet silhouette of her form. Dive now saw only her hands as dark amethyst. Had she been taller, he would have known her to be Mael's mate, but she stood too short to be Rosealise.

Nellie Quinn. Seeing her creep toward the barn flooded Kiaran with sharp satisfaction. *What do you now, you wee impostor?*

He sent a command to Dive to shadow the American, and then rushed down the stairs and out through the tower's arch. He found Domnall alone banking the fires in the great hall, and gave him the hand signal for an unknown intruder sighted. It wasn't precisely correct, but he needed the chieftain to catch the wench at her mischief. That would serve as his proof.

Domnall tossed him a sword, and followed him out of the stronghold at a fast, silent run.

Kiaran pointed to where Dive had last seen the wench, and then used hunting signals for them to split apart, flank the barn and come at her from either side. The chieftain wordlessly agreed by tapping his chest before he followed the ambling curve of the curtain wall. Kiaran did the same in the opposite direction.

He smelled a flowery scent just before he came upon her from behind, and snatched at the back of Jenna's hood to reveal her small head of gilded curls. Nellie spun around, a dagger ready in her hand, and then with a quick movement tried to conceal it under the cloak.

"Say naught," Kiaran said as her lips parted, and leveled his own blade even with her thin throat. "On your knees. Join your hands behind your neck. Now."

Domnall came up behind her, and as soon as he realized it was Nellie sheathed his sword. "Mistress Quinn, I reckoned you abed."

She tipped her head back and smiled at him before she regarded Kiaran and arched her brows.

"I forbid her speak," he told the chieftain as Dive soared down to perch on his gauntlet. "Any word she utters shall be wrapped in lies."

The kestrel made a sharp sound, but directed it at her master, not Nellie.

"By the Gods." Mael, who emerged from the back of the keepe and came to stand beside Domnall, gaped at the wench. "Mistress Quinn, what do you out here this time of night?"

"Follow her tracks," the chieftain told him. "I want to ken where she's been. Kiaran, put away your sword now." He reached down and took hold of Nellie's hands, taking them from her neck and tugging her to her feet. "You may speak to me, Mistress, and explain your presence outside the stronghold."

"I couldn't sleep," she said, her tone one of innocent confusion. "I thought I'd take a little walk until I got tired." She pushed out her lips to pout. "Sorry, but I'm a bit of a night owl, you know."

"A walk to weary yourself." Kiaran uttered a sour laugh. "With a dagger at your hip, and Jenna's garments on your back."

"I borrowed the clothes from the laundry. I don't have much to wear, and I didn't think she would mind." She produced the dagger, and offered it to the chieftain. "Edane gave me the blade. He said I should carry it with me all the time, just in case the demon comes back for me."

"An excuse for everything you do." Kiaran spat on the ground. "As ever."

"Say, I get that you don't like me very much," Nellie said to him, sounding forlorn now. "Whatever I did to peeve you, I'm sorry. But I'm not spying for the Sluath, see? That one was hunting me when Danny came to my rescue, remember?"

"Or so you claimed. Mayhap the demon

wanted Edane to believe that, so he would bring you here." Kiaran saw Mael returning with a bulging satchel in his grip, and nodded toward him. "I reckon you unmasked now, Mistress. Admit why you came to Dun Chaill."

She shrugged. "Edane brought me."

The seneschal handed the traveling pack to Domnall. "I found this in the stables, beside a saddled mare. I reckon she went there some hours past, likely from the kitchens while she prepared the brews for us."

"You're a good tracker, Man Mountain." Nellie sighed as she pulled off the cloak and held it out to the chieftain. "Shame you can't see what's right in front of your nose."

When Domnall reached for Jenna's garment, the wench tossed it in his face, dodged between him and Mael, and fled toward the gardens.

Kiaran swore as he went after her, surprised anew by her speed. She ran as sure-footed as a deer, even with the too-big tartan gown flapping around her legs. As she followed the curtain wall, she kept reaching out to touch it with her hand, and then abruptly stopped and walked into the ashlar. As soon as he reached the spot where she had disappeared, he saw the shimmer of dark blue light, and the yawning gap of stones folding back on themselves.

"Mistress, stop," he shouted. When she didn't show herself, he drew his blade and ran through the portal.

On the other side of the arch he saw a long, dark passage, and the blur of movement at the other end. Torches flared to life along the curving walls, each billowing brighter as their flames swelled. Acrid smoke rose to pelt the rounded ceiling like a writhing, gray-fleeced sheep. Stones began to melt, revealing themselves to be rotted wood under the cracking, blackening paint. The blocks caught flame from the torches, and blazed as if soaked with oil.

"Get out of here." Nellie hurried toward him, pushing him frantically toward the portal. "It's all going to go up. Hurry."

Yet when Kiaran turned, the arch in the wall closed again, trapping them both in the tunnel of flames.

Chapter Fourteen

GALAN PLACED FIANA'S bones beside his bed in the corner of the barn, emerging from the niche once he had covered the bag with his cloak. Tonight, he would sleep beside his wife for the first time in twelve centuries. Even if he couldn't take her in his arms, breathe in her scent and listen to the soft music of her voice, he'd take comfort in knowing that soon he would.

All he had to do was find Iolar's half-brother.

"You should drink," Danar said as he emptied the dregs from the bottle of whiskey into a cup, and handed it to him. "You're still mortal enough to enjoy spirits."

"'Twill but give me a sore head in the morning." Galan absently took a sip as he stared at the long rows of blades the demon had set out on a work table. Each night Danar removed and sharpened every weapon he carried, as part of some private ritual unfathomable to the druid. "I wish to ride out at dawn to begin my search for the halfling. Where did you look for him after he escaped?"

"He used the same gate in the ridges by that village you raided." The big demon took out his palm stone, dampening it before he began plying a throwing dagger against it. "When you named the magic that was used to seal it, I thought perhaps it had been the work of the halfling. The king sired him on a Pritani slave."

"Why didnae you tell me that?" Before Danar could answer Galan worked it out. "You couldnae, else the prince would learn of your deception."

"I sensed no Sluath presence near the gate but our own. The halfling still leaves a trace of that." Metal scraped against the whetstone with a harsh sound. "You cannot track him after a thousand years gone. He left no trace there. I also recall that our prince ordered you to find the touch-reader."

Galan picked up a bronze knife with a handle carved from yellowed mortal bone. "'Tis aimless to chase after this wench. If he wishes treasure, he may send the demons to raid one of the great clan holds. They've enough gold and jewels to satisfy a king."

"Ah, but this treasure has no equal." Danar tested the edge of the dagger before sheathing it and selected another. "Besides that, Nellie Quinn is more useful to us than the halfling. She's not gone mad."

Galan put down the knife before he gave into the urge to ram it into the demon's throat. "I dinnae care what you want of her."

"She can read the past from any object she touches." When he didn't reply Danar laughed. "Think for once beyond your desires, druid. Once we have her, Nellie can be made to read any of the closed gates. Once she does, she can tell you the exact spell that was used to seal it."

Now he understood. "If I ken the spell, I may reopen the gate to the underworld."

"Making you the most valuable of Prince

Iolar's subjects. Being trapped here is driving him as mad as the halfling." The demon regarded him directly. "Understand something else: Nellie is my most prized cull. Her power has been hers since birth, and she used it to live an exceptionally wicked life. I then invested nearly a century in tormenting the remnants of her humanity out of her. She's unique among mortals."

Galan picked up on the pride in Danar's tone. "You sound as a doting sire would."

The demon's coppery eyes glinted. "As a king I begat dozens of daughters on my wives, my concubines and my slaves. Some were lovely, others clever, and a few even exceeded my expectations and became powerful wives to important rulers. None, however, came close to being the woman Nellie is."

"You loved her." He glanced up at the hayloft. "I thought the *deamhanan* incapable of such feeling."

"We are." Danar went back to sharpening his blade. "Yet I remember love as a mortal. If I were still capable of it, I would have adored her."

Something in his tone made Galan take a step back. "But no more."

"The little bitch betrayed me. She made me look the fool before our prince. No mortal in either of my lives has ever so thoroughly routed me." He stretched out his wings, making the blade sheaths strapped to them bristle like blunt quills. "I look forward to seeing her again, druid."

He almost felt sorry for the wench. "What shall you do with her?"

"She stole the prince's most prized possession, deceived us all, and escaped the underworld. Never has there been such a mortal." Danar drove the blade in his hand deep into the wooden table. "For that she shall suffer the torments of ten thousand years."

Chapter Fifteen

BRODEN RAN TO the great hall as soon as he heard Rosealise's call for help. He found her lugging one of the fire buckets toward a murky cloud between two of the hearths, but neither held flame.

"Here," the housekeeper said, dashing the sand from the bucket against the stones. More streams of smoke wafted out from the seams as she turned to him. "I think the fire may be inside the wall."

"Stand back," he told her as he touched the stones, which felt red-hot in an area as tall as he stood. He drew back his fist, and used his gift of inhuman power to hit the wall. The rock exploded, and blood dripped from his knuckles as he struck again at the spot.

The stone cracked and fell away, and thick smoke and flames jetted out, driving Broden back. Rosealise handed him another bucket of sand, which he threw at the blazing gap. Through it he could now see a passage engulfed in fire, and the silhouettes of two figures, one tall and the other petite.

Dive flew into the hall and began hovering above the hole and screeching frantically, telling him who one of the trapped was.

"Kiaran, to me," Broden shouted, and tugged at the ragged edge of the gap until he made an opening large enough for them to squeeze through into the hall.

The falconer, his head covered by his smoldering tartan, appeared on the other side. He pushed through a cloak-wrapped bundle, which Broden grabbed and dragged out. Kiaran tore off his tartan before he shouldered his way into the gap, seizing the bundle again and tearing the cloak from a soot-covered, coughing Nellie Quinn.

Broden saw the flames inside the hidden passage abruptly extinguish, leaving only smoke to pour through the gap.

"How did you get inside the wall?"

Rosealise asked, putting her arm around Nellie.

She coughed harshly before she said, "I saw…an arch…and ducked…in it."

Broden saw Kiaran's face and stepped between him and the gasping female. "Never, Brother."

"I caught the wench sneaking out of the keepe," the falconer told him. "When Domnall and I confronted her, she ran from us. She's been sent by the Sluath to spy on us."

Broden glanced at Nellie, whose expression grew bewildered before she shook her head.

"Perhaps there has been some terrible misunderstanding," Rosealise said, sounding unconvinced of her own words. "I think we should have the chieftain to sort this out."

"I agree," Domnall said as he and Mael strode in from the kitchens. He glanced around the haze of smoke and the hole Broden had punched in the wall. "'Twould seem you sprang another trap, Kiaran."

"No' me. The wench did." The falconer glared at Nellie. "She lured me inside."

"You chased me into it," she countered,

and cleared her throat. "It only caught fire after the arch closed."

By then Jenna and Edane had joined them, and the archer rushed to Nellie's side, halting only when Mael caught his arm.

"Release me," Edane demanded. "I must see to her injuries."

"Wait a moment, lad," the seneschal warned him after he exchanged a look with Domnall. "Give the lass a chance to speak."

"I'm all right. I just breathed in some smoke, that's all," Nellie told him. "Kiaran wrapped me up and carried me through the flames." To the falconer, she said, "Thank you."

"Dinnae offer me your sham gratitude." Kiaran seized the satchel from Mael's hand and emptied it at Nellie's feet, spilling food and waterskins on the floor. "You wished proof, Chieftain, and 'tis before you now. Hadnae I spied her skulking away, she'd have stolen that horse as well."

Edane went still. "What?"

Broden rubbed his smoke-stung eyes for a moment. He'd suspected something amiss with Nellie, but the archer had been entirely blinded by her charm and beauty. To see this must have felt for Edane like a blade to the belly.

"So 'twould seem." Domnall regarded the lass. "Why did you steal from us, Mistress?"

She moved her shoulders. "I don't know anything about this bag or a horse. I was just going for a walk outside." Her expression hardened as she eyed Kiaran. "Say, maybe you should ask him. Wouldn't be hard to make it look like I did this, see."

Outrage made the falconer's eyes go deadly. "You dare blame your trickery on me?"

"You've wanted me gone since I got here, pal," the lass countered. "Maybe this is the way you figured would get rid of me for good, huh?"

The air crackled with leashed violence about to spill. Broden couldn't tell from Nellie's face or eyes if she spoke the truth, but he knew someone who could.

"Chieftain, mayhap Lady Rosealise should speak with the lass."

"Aye." Domnall glanced at the housekeeper. "My lady, if you're willing?"

The housekeeper's mouth flattened, but she reluctantly nodded and went to Nellie.

"Forgive me for this, my dear," Rosealise said as she touched the younger woman's arm. "Please answer our questions truthfully."

Nellie stiffened, and then spoke in a tight, halting voice. "I stole the food and water. Jenna's clothes, too. I would have taken the horse. I needed them to get away."

Kiaran made a contemptuous sound, while Edane stared at her as if she'd spat in his face.

"Where meant you to go, and why?" Domnall asked.

"Anywhere far from this place." Her thin hands twisted together, but the housekeeper's persuasion power made her add, "I don't want to die here."

"We've done naught but make you welcome," Edane said slowly, as if the words pained him. "You knew I'd protect you from the Sluath. The clan meant to keep you safe."

"You don't understand." Nellie stared at her scorched slippers. "It's nothing to do with you or the clan. I…I had no choice. I couldn't stay here."

"I never threatened the wench," Kiaran said to no one in particular, as if accused of the same.

"Will you just shut up for a minute?" Jenna said, and came over to join the women. "Nellie, why were you afraid to stay here? Was it because of Kiaran?"

"No. They made this place to kill us." She looked at Edane. "I'm sorry. I wanted to take you with me, but I was afraid they'd find out if they saw more than one go missing."

"They?" The chieftain's wife frowned. "Who do you mean?"

This time Nellie visibly fought answering, even clapping her hand over her mouth to muffle the answer she had been compelled to speak.

"Take your hand away and tell us, Miss Quinn," Rosealise said gently.

Her fingers slid from her lips. "The Sluath. This place, they built it. It's not a castle. It's a prison."

Broden felt a chill run through him. "How can you ken that, my lady?"

Tears spilled down Nellie's face. "When I touch things, I see where they came from, and what happened around them, like a moving picture. The walls showed me the monster that built this place. He's like the demons, only ugly and scarred and crazy." She wrung her hands. "Don't you see? We never left the underworld. They just made us think we did with their magic. We're still slaves, and this is more torture. This is where they're going to kill us."

"My dear girl." Rosealise took her hand away from her arm. "You're quite wrong. We did escape, all of us. There are no demons here. Dun Chaill is a relic, not a prison."

"I knew you wouldn't believe me," the flapper said, wrapping her arms around herself and peering at the walls as if she expected them to collapse. "That's why I had to run. Now they'll come and kill us all." Her voice broke on a sob.

"That's not happening. I promise." Jenna put her arms around the weeping lass, and exchanged a look with her husband before she said, "Nellie, do you know how much time has passed since Dun Chaill was built by this monster?"

The flapper wiped at her wet face. "I don't

know, a couple of months, maybe a year. What does that matter?"

"It's been over a thousand years since anyone lived at Dun Chaill," the chieftain's wife said gently. "It's true that the Sluath probably used this as a trap when the Mag Raith came here in their mortal lives, but that was twelve hundred years ago."

"We're immortal, lass," Broden said gently. "We've been thus since we escaped the underworld. Our ladies both died and came back to us the same."

Jenna nodded at the lass's incredulous look. "Just to be completely honest, there are still some old traps in place around the castle, as you just found out. As soon as we find them, we either disarm them or seal them off so they can't hurt us."

Nellie scrubbed at her wet eyes. "Why didn't you tell me any of this?"

Edane answered that question in a toneless voice. "We didnae trust you." He turned and stalked out of the hall.

Broden saw the lass's shoulders slump, and said to Rosealise, "Mayhap we should put

Kiaran's suspicions to rest now, and finish this."

The housekeeper nodded, and rested her hand on Nellie's shoulder. "Did the Sluath send you here to spy for them, Miss Quinn?"

"I don't think so." The flapper took in a shuddering breath. "But I don't know for sure. I can't remember what they did to me."

Chapter Sixteen

IN HIS CHAMBER, Edane went directly to the bed. At its end, Nellie's gown and shift lay draped over the edge. The entire place still smelled of her elusive sweetness, and everywhere he looked he saw some reminder of her. The strips of his tartan she'd used to adorn herself she'd wound neatly in coils on a shelf. The half-drunk mug of whiskey-laced brew she'd made him, still sitting on his table. Even the shape of her lay beneath his blanket.

He yanked back the wool cover, revealing the fleeces she'd used to stuff it. She had expected him to look in on her, and left this to make him believe she still occupied his bed. As he stared at this undeniable show of treachery,

Edane wondered if anything about Nellie had been genuine.

The door opened behind him, and Broden came to survey the assembled fleeces. "A convincing sham. She's a clever one, your lass."

Edane sat down and picked up an arrow to be fletched. "Aye, so clever she deceived us all, and near burned Kiaran alive. She's no my lass, and I've been a blind fool. What more would you crow at me?"

"You left before Rosealise asked if she spies for the Sluath. Nellie couldnae recall." Broden gathered up the fleeces and stuffed them in a basket. "I reckon no', else they'd have compelled her to signal them somehow to come for us. I'll wager she meant only to escape what she believed a demon prison, and stole to provision herself for the journey. No' unlike as we did when we left the Moss Dapple."

He met the trapper's gaze. "You defend what she's done?"

"We concealed as much from her as she did from us. Kiaran's spitefulness toward the lass didnae help." He paused. "You'll soon snap that." Broden took the arrow creaking in his tight fingers and set it aside. "I reckon in her place, with what she saw, I might have fled."

"What did Domnall with her?" Edane hated himself for asking, but he had to know.

"Jenna made up a bed for her in the old pantry. I blocked the doors so she cannae get out again." The trapper crossed his arms over chest. "What would you have from the lass, Brother?"

"Naught." Edane felt offended by the suggestion. "Nellie doesnae care for me or anyone but herself. All she said to me, 'twas but more lies."

"Likely why she asked me to tell you again that she's sorry, through the pantry door as I set the barricades." Broden smiled a little. "Likely she did so that she might dupe you once more into…" He paused and rubbed his chin. "Do you ken, I cannae fathom Nellie's purpose in coddling your affections. Did she filch your bows? Wheedle from you some waterskins? Take your pouch of baubles?"

Edane eyed his brother. "I showed her the way to leave. I told her how we came to the castle. She took from me all she needed to escape."

The trapper nodded. "Aye, truly evil work. For that I'll have Kiaran beat her in the morn, and you may watch, to delight in the suffering she so richly deserves."

"Enough." Edane felt even more foolish now. "I've but myself to blame for growing attached to the lass. I thought better of her, and my pride's bruised. But aye, I'll stop being a facking wench about it. 'Twill satisfy you?"

"I'd have a truth that wasnae spoken tonight." Broden gave him a measuring look. "You recall the lure Nectan bid us use on that old stag who kept trampling our snares and raiding the gardens?"

"A young hind in rut."

The hunt he referred to had been ordered by Domnall's father, who had wanted the stag's magnificent curving antlers to adorn his *broch*. They had used the breeding female to lure the old rascal into a valley, and then, curiously, Domnall had refused to end him. He'd instead chased the stag out of their lands.

"I'm to take charge of the lass on the morrow," the trapper said. "I'll teach her to tend to the cows in the morning, put out a lure, and learn what I may."

Edane hated the idea, but shrugged to show his indifference. "What matters that to me?"

Broden smiled. "You'll be watching as I do."

Chapter Seventeen

⚜

THE ROOM WHERE Domnall and Jenna had put Nellie had no windows, but as she woke, she felt the light of dawn inside, as if her body knew the sun had risen. Tired and defeated, she sat up on the blanket-padded pallet and waited for her eyes to adjust to the thin darkness.

Back behind the eight ball again.

The chieftain's wife had spoken at length with her before they'd barricaded her inside, and now she felt like a dimwit for everything she'd assumed from her touch visions. But Jenna had been kind, if a bit more reserved with her, and insisted that the Mag Raith wouldn't hurt her for stealing and lying to them.

"Domnall's not happy about the situation," the architect admitted. "We're also concerned about how the Sluath may have tampered with your memory. If you do recall anything about the underworld, you should tell me now. It could help a lot in figuring out how we should move forward."

Telling Jenna about the vision she had shared with Edane during their petting party had made Nellie cringe. But she was sure the archer would have already let the others know about it, and she had no reason to keep lying now.

Instead of disgusting the other woman, her memories seemed to reassure her.

"We think the Sluath gave me and Rosealise to Domnall and Mael as bed slaves," Jenna said, astounding her. "So, it's just the reverse with you and Edane. The fact is that you two did meet in the underworld, and had feelings for each other." She frowned. "I wonder why they didn't treat Edane like the other hunters."

"He was sick, I think," Nellie told her. "In the vision he looked much thinner and kind of frail, too, even before the big one beat him. I said something about his chest, like he had an injury." She ducked her head. "I should have tried to stop Danar from hurting him."

"You probably would have gotten a beating, too," the other woman said as she picked up the lantern. "Nellie, until we get to the bottom of this, we're going to keep you here at Dun Chaill. I don't like it, but it seems like the best way to keep everyone safe."

"And when you find out why I was dumped in the glen?" she countered. "What happens to me then?"

"By then maybe you'll want to stay." With a smile Jenna left.

Now outside the door Nellie heard someone moving a heavy weight, and it opened to reveal Rosealise with a clean gown and a lantern.

"I thought you might like to change before breakfast." The housekeeper placed the dress beside her.

"That's nice. Thanks." Nellie saw the gown had been tailored to fit her, and looked up at Rosealise. "If you need me to do some mending while I'm in here… I mean, I think I can sew pretty well." It would also help pass the time until they decided what they were going to do with her.

"I'm told that the chieftain has other plans for you today." Rosealise hesitated before she said, "I don't believe in holding grudges, Miss Quinn. You need not worry that I will treat you any differently than I have in the past."

"What about Edane?" Nellie grimaced. "Sorry, I shouldn't keep asking about him."

"Perhaps you should give him some time to sort out his feelings," the housekeeper suggested before she stepped out.

Once Nellie had dressed Rosealise walked with her into the great hall, where everyone but Kiaran and Edane sat gathered around the trestle table. No one said anything as she joined them, but Jenna smiled at her. Domnall then spoke with Mael about permanently sealing off the fire trap passage at both ends, which Jenna proposed doing with grates until they determined what triggered the flames and how they could disarm it.

"I'd have you work with Broden on tending the livestock today, Mistress Quinn," Domnall said, startling her. "Or you may remain at your leisure in the pantry. I shallnae force you to work."

Nellie liked the trapper, and being locked up all day had little appeal. "Sure, I'll help."

After they finished the morning meal Broden escorted Nellie out to the barn, where a half-dozen cows stood waiting in their stanchions. From the look of their swollen udders they needed milking, so after he handed her a long apron to wear, she rolled up her sleeves and washed her hands at the basin stand.

"We'll see to the cows, and then weed the herb garden for Rosealise." The trapper took down a bucket and three-legged stool from a shelf and went to the first stall, where he patted the heifer's shoulder. "Come and I'll show you how to milk her."

"I think I've got this." Nellie positioned the stool by the cow before tucking the bucket between her shins and stroking the animal's side. It felt like the right way, and she watched the legs before she took the wet, soapy rag Broden handed her. Using it to clean the udder and teats seemed simple enough, as did drying them with the bottom of her apron. "Say, you got some balm?"

The words were out of her before she'd even realized she'd asked. Though Broden's brows arched, he nodded and produced a little stone jar that he gave to her. For a moment she stared at it.

How did I know to ask for it? In fact, how do I know anything about–

Her temple twinged, making her wince.

Never mind. Don't try to remember. Just do what comes naturally.

Nellie rubbed some of the salve on her palms and sat down. When she realized she couldn't reach the udder she scooted up so close she had to turn her head. As she rested her cheek against the cow she felt for the swollen teats.

"Good girl," she murmured as she began tugging and squeezing, finding the right grip to use. Heavy streams of milk soon hissed against the side of the pail. "You're just full of it today, aren't you?"

The trapper watched her for a while before he retrieved another stool and went to the next stall.

Nellie breathed in the scent of warm milk, which sweetened the straw-musty air, and then detected a slight sour note. "Brodie, you boys raking up the dirt after you muck out the stalls in here?"

Broden glanced over his shoulder. "Why? 'Tis dirt."

"It's dirt you've been soaking with a lot of spilled milk," she corrected. "With the summer coming pretty soon it's going to reek in here. Also, you should keep one hand on your bucket in case the cow moves or kicks. That stops most of the splashes and spills."

The trapper just grunted and went back to milking.

Once they finished with all the cows and carried the pails into the buttery, Nellie strained hers through a sack into a clean basin and covered it.

"That spotted heifer looks like they barned her too long," she mentioned as they walked back outside. "She's got hard feet. You'll need to cut down her hooves and watch them for cracks."

Turning out the docile cows to graze proved easy, as they ambled out of the barn's open pasture doors as soon as Nellie and Broden released them. She went along to take a better look at the herd, which looked well-fed and healthy, and noted the number of calves. The bull standing toward the outside of the herd swung his head around to inspect them before returning his attention to the lush grass.

"Where are you watering them, down at the stream?" she asked, and Broden nodded. "That's fine for now, but you're going to need to build some troughs for when it freezes in winter."

The trapper eyed her. "How many?"

She glanced at the herd as she calculated. "If you size them for three, and build one for every fifty head… Five deep troughs should be plenty. But you'll need to separate the herd. Once the calves get bigger, you have to pen the bulls away from each other and the heifers until it's time to breed them."

It seemed obvious to her but the look on Broden's face said it was anything but. Again she resisted the urge to remember how she knew.

He gestured for her to follow him back into the barn, where he closed the doors and bolted them. Nellie watched as he poured some fresh water into a basin.

Why did he lock the doors? Washing up beside him, Nellie tried to shrug off the sense of being trapped. Then she caught the way he was looking at her. *Oh, he's got plans for me.*

"You ken much of cattle," Broden mentioned as he held out a clean swatch of linen. When she tried to take it, he caught her hands in it, and held them. "Too much for a lass who dwelled in town."

"Yeah, I guess. Can't remember." She also suspected that the chieftain hadn't told him to do this. Still, Broden didn't look like he wanted to beat the tar out of her, so it had to be something else. "You got a problem with that?"

"Jenna told us of your New York City," the trapper said as he began gently drying her hands. "'Tis filled with many strange and wondrous things, but no' cattle or dairy farms."

"Maybe I lived in the country." She tried to pull away, but he wouldn't let go of her. "Something else you wanted?"

"Aye." He dropped the linen and stroked his thumbs along the insides of her wrists. The touch felt light but definitely more than friendly. "You're a worldly lass. I've no' taken a lover since here we came. We neither of us wish entanglements."

This she'd almost been expecting, and still she felt disappointed. "So you know all about me now, huh?"

"I'd ken more." He leaned close, grazing her cheek with his as he put his mouth next to her ear. "Come up into the loft," he murmured, his rasping voice like a rough caress. "We've hours before anyone misses us."

Nellie sighed. With the charm Broden was pouring on it would be easy to give in. He had that look of a guy who could make a girl's toes curl, and she bet she knew plenty of ways to twist his. He'd definitely take her mind off her troubles, and he was right. Who would know? But all she could think of was Edane, and the wounded look in his eyes when Rosealise had forced the truth out of her.

"I'd be loony not to, huh?" She gave his hands a fond squeeze before she stepped back. "Can't do that to Danny, pal. Sorry."

"You believe the archer shall forgive you

for deceiving us?" Broden sounded skeptical now. "You dinnae ken my brother."

"Yeah, yeah, I'm a liar and Edane hates me. I got that last night." She rubbed the ink on the back of her neck, which felt uncomfortably hot for a moment. "Doesn't change how I feel."

"You've feelings." He chuckled as if she'd made a joke. "Aye, and you'd have run from Dun Chaill without a word of warning to him or any of us about what you reckoned would end the clan. 'Tis touching, how greatly you care."

So that was what they thought of her. Fair enough. Only it made her angry, so angry she thought she might slap his fine face. Then the truth just poured out of her.

"You ever been so scared you can't remember to breathe?" Nellie nodded as his smirk faded. "Sweat running down your back, hands shaking, head full of screaming that nobody but you can hear? You can't hear anything else. Everything crowds in on you. You'd peel your own skin off to get away. That's what I felt from the minute I walked in this joint and saw that thing that built it. I didn't know any of you, see? You could have been in on it."

Broden nodded. "Truth."

He'd been through something just as bad. Nellie could see it now in his pretty eyes. Someone had done a number on the trapper, and she'd bet he sometimes still heard the screaming, just like she did.

"We're a lot alike, you and me. We do what we have to so we can get by." She saw him flinch. "Hey, that doesn't make us heartless."

"No?" He didn't sound convinced.

"Trust me, I got one in here somewhere." She poked a finger at her chest. "Might be the size of a peanut, and frozen stiff, but it still works. Maybe yours does, too, because I think you wouldn't have asked me if you didn't care. You'd have just taken what you wanted, right?"

"As you say." Broden touched her face, and when he took his fingers away, they looked wet. "Forgive me, my lady." He bowed to her like she was some bigshot.

Nellie laughed at him. "Come on, let's get at the garden."

Chapter Eighteen

ONCE BRODEN AND Nellie left the stock barn Edane jumped down from where he'd watched them. His brother had warned him that the lass might accept his lure of seduction, and he'd been prepared for that. Instead she'd shown herself as someone entirely different: an honorable female who cared more for him than the prospect of pleasure and comfort that Broden had offered her.

Likely 'twas all deception.

Nellie might have realized he was hidden there, and sought to mislead him again. Or she had been ingratiating herself with the trapper, in hopes of gaining some sway over him.

Edane left through the pasture door, and found Kiaran standing outside. Above him Dive perched on one of the barn windows, making it obvious why he had come.

"Broden told you what he meant to do?"

"No." The falconer held up his gauntlet, and the kestrel flew down to perch on it. He stroked Dive's small head as he looked over toward the kitchen garden. "I but wondered if she'd attempt to flee again once outside the keepe. Instead she plays dairy maid as if born to milk. I marvel at the scope of her skills."

"As you saw, Nellie didnae run." The last thing he wanted was to clash with Kiaran, especially after he had been proven right in his suspicions. "Mayhap you should attend to your forge now, Brother."

The falconers dark eyes narrowed. "Dinnae trifle with the wench, Edane. She's no' worthy of you."

Was he such a prize, then? Edane wondered as he watched the falconer stride off. In the vision he had shared with Nellie, the oversize demon had spoken of him as worthless for all but facking and slaughter. Since becoming immortal he had attained the strength and vigor enjoyed by the other Mag Raith, but he never forgot how he'd felt the first time they'd come to Dun Chaill.

For which I damned us all.

His palm throbbed, and Edane glanced down to see his own hand flattened against his chest, as he'd often done before their last hunt. Beneath the flesh and bone his heart pumped with slow, even beats, powerful and sure, and seemingly never to stop.

As it had never beat in his mortal life.

In boyhood the strange fluttering in his chest when he ran more than a few steps had often caused Edane to lose his breath. By comparison he knew himself to be different from the other lads, but never spoke of the spells to anyone. Still, his parents had seen his weakness. His sire refused to train him as a warrior, and his *máthair* forbid him do all but the lightest of women's work. As Edane grew older his resentment over their coddling swelled, especially when they had given him to the tribe's shaman for training.

The Gods dinnae bestow a gift to see it thus squandered, lad, the old man had told him when he'd tried to refuse his teachings.

From long habit Edane pushed away the unhappy memories and went to work in the greenhouse. The herbs and veg starters he'd been cultivating now thrived, and would soon be ready for planting in Rosealise's kitchen garden. Since he had no desire to face Nellie he walked the perimeter of the spell boundary to check its condition, but found no sign of breaches. All the while he thought on the previous night's events, and he thought on every word Nellie had been compelled to speak. Kiaran's warning had been justified, but what had they learned of the lass, other than she had concealed her touch-reading power?

I truly ken naught about her but that she fears the Sluath and Dun Chaill.

Once he'd finished his patrol Edane made his way into the stronghold, intent on preparing the fire trap opening in the great hall for the grate Domnall wished to install. Once there he found himself staring at the black-edged hole Broden had punched through the wall.

Why didnae I notice it?

Of the hunters only he and Mael could

see the traces left by the use of magic. Last night he had been so focused on Nellie that he hadn't even bothered to inspect the trap. Now he could see a shimmer at the far end of the passage, and some fragments glowing at the base of the torches, but nothing on the scorched wooden walls. The bespelled opening had led Kiaran and Nellie into the passage, and closed behind them, but magic had not set it alight.

"Just when I believe we have this household in hand, we find another reason to worry," Rosealise's brisk voice said from behind him.

"'Tis no' like the others we've discovered," Edane said as he leaned closer and breathed in. He detected the particular stink of charred fat, and noted the odd appearance of the wall panels. "The fire burned through thin wood panels to what seems a foundation of stone. 'Twas meant to burn hot, but briefly. 'Twould kill an intruder, but prevent the fire from spreading to the rest of the stronghold."

"Egad, how gruesome." She pressed a hand against the base of her throat. "I never think of the purpose behind these wretched traps. They simply terrify me."

What she said brought to mind all the work he had seen Broden do over the centuries. Lures had to be fresh, but so did the makings. Had this passage been built a thousand years past, the fat would have long ago dissolved, and the wood used to fashion the torches rotted to dust. Magic might have preserved them, but he saw no sign of that. Everything told him that the fire trap had been set far more recently, perhaps in the last several days.

He stepped back to see the trap with fresh eyes.

"Edane," the housekeeper said quietly into the silence, "might I have a word with you?"

For a moment he'd forgotten she was still there. Then he realized that she must have come looking for him.

"My apologies, my lady," he said, turning to her. "Please have your say."

"I believe that Miss Quinn is still hiding something from us. I feel it quite strongly. I have also informed the chieftain that I will not again compel her to do anything against her will. If we are to convince her that we mean her no harm, we must encourage her trust."

He didn't have to ask why. Rosealise felt using her persuasion power was akin to a personal violation. "How may we convince her to confide it, then?"

"I think you should ask her that question. You'll find her in her room now, working on some mending for Broden." She gave him a reassuring smile before she went back into the kitchens.

Edane knew that speaking with the lass tempted trouble. She had deceived him so easily that he yet bristled at the thought, but his feet took him down the passage toward the old pantry. This time Broden had not barricaded the door, although Domnall would likely order him to for the night. Once the chieftain lost his trust in anyone, he rarely offered it again.

Edane stopped outside, lifting his hand to knock. A peculiar cracking sound from within made him yank the door open.

Nellie looked up from a pair of trews that she was patching, and her eyes rounded. "Danny?"

As a deep rumble shook the pantry, Edane lunged at her. He seized her and covered her with his body as the wall behind her collapsed on top of them.

※

Rocks and dirt pelted Nellie as Edane struggled against the pile of stone on top of them. More stones fell, burying them deeper. Her body hurt in a dozen places, but she could feel the warmth of blood dripping down on her arms and legs, and knew it wasn't hers. She should have held her breath and kept her eyes closed, but the frantic need to know if he was still alive made her writhe as she tried to turn under him.

"Danny." Debris fell against her face as she gasped his name, and the dust grew thicker. "Edane, don't you dare die on me."

"I yet live, my *peyrl*," he said, his voice muffled against her hair. "Be still. The clan shall soon come and free us."

"You shouldn't have done that." She spat some dirt from her mouth. "Why didn't you just stay clear?"

"You wouldnae look so lovely crushed," he said. "Didnae you hear the stones shifting while you worked?"

"No." She'd been so shocked to see him rushing in that a demon could have dropped on her head and she wouldn't have noticed. "I thought you guys rebuilt this place."

"Here all but the ceiling 'twas intact when we came." His arms tightened around her as shouts came from above. "You see? My brothers come."

"Mistress Quinn?" she heard Domnall shout.

Edane called back to him. "I have her. She lives. We're beside the pallet."

She heard the chieftain speaking to someone else, and Mael swearing softly as the weight shifted again, pinning her feet.

"My God, stop," Jenna said, her anxious voice growing louder. "You could crush them. Don't touch anything else until I take a look."

Long moments of silence passed, and Nellie wondered if the Mag Raith would be able to dig them out.

"If I don't make it, will you take me somewhere else to bury me?" She sniffed back some tears. "Like maybe that glen where we met? That was pretty."

"You shallnae die today, lass." Somehow Edane managed to caress her arm with his fingers. "I promise you."

"Edane, we have to move two beams before we can start digging you out," Jenna called through the pile. "It might disturb the rubble, so do what you can to protect her head and chest."

"He's on top of me, sister," Nellie called back to her. "Protect him, why don't you?"

The architect uttered a strange laugh. "Okay, we'll do our best. Hang on."

What followed seemed even scarier than the wall dropping on them. More dirt and then bits of thatching fell through the stones as the men began to work. Wood groaned and cracked, and heavy weights thudded all around them. She felt her eyes sting, and then Edane began murmuring words of reassurance.

"Remember, my lady, we survived the underworld and the Sluath," he told her, his breath warm against her nape. "'Tis but some stone and mortar and wood. Naught for my brothers to clear. They'll reach us soon, I swear it."

She thought of what she'd been doing. "Broden's trousers are probably rags now."

"'Tis what he deserves for no' mending them himself, the lazy arse," the archer assured her.

Air and light began to filter into the heavy pile around them, and then stones began to fall away as grimy hands appeared, reaching for more to pull away.

"We can see where you are now," Jenna said, her hand working in to touch Nellie's shoulder. "Just stay right there. Domnall, use that tree limb to lever that last column away that's pinning them down. That's the way."

Finally, Nellie could see the men digging through the stone. Mael moved huge swaths of rubble with his arms, as if he were swimming through the pile. Broden and Kiaran were wedging posts upright, and she glanced up to see most of the roofing had gone, and the walls above the pantry had fallen in on them as well.

Domnall appeared over them, his powerful arms bunching as he lifted them both from the remainder of the debris. Nellie turned and saw Edane's grimy face, and then nearly fainted at the sight of his blood-soaked tunic and trousers.

"Forget about me," she told the chieftain as he hefted them clear of the wreckage of the room. "You save him."

"I'm immortal, lass," the archer reminded her as he stood and nodded to Domnall before he swept her up in his arms. He carried her out of the pantry, stepping over more stones as he made his way down the hazy passage. When he reached his chamber, he kicked the door open and brought her in to his bed.

"I'm bleeding all over," she warned him, but the fierce look in his eyes convinced her to stay put. "You don't have to do this for me. You're really banged up."

"I'll live." He checked her eyes and face and looked all over her front before turning her onto her side and checking her back. His hands gently moved along her spine, her arms and her legs before he covered her with his blanket. "You've some small wounds that want cleaning and binding, but I feel no bones broken."

"Thanks to you, fella." She tried to sit up, but her arms felt as if filled with jelly. As he tore off the shreds of his tunic, she said, "Let me see your back now."

His mouth hitched as he turned, and Nellie cried out as she saw the bloody gashes and dark bruises crisscrossing his spine.

"You carried me like that?" she demanded, pushing herself off the bed. Yet even as she reached out to him the wounds began to shrink. "What the devil?"

"'Tis another gift bestowed by our immortality. We heal very quickly." Edane turned around as Mael and his wife appeared in the doorway. "Lady Rosealise, would you tend to Mistress Quinn's injuries? I must help the others." When she nodded, he smiled and strode out.

The seneschal heaved a sigh of relief. "You gave us a proper scare this time, lass."

"I didn't do anything, I swear," Nellie assured him. "I was just sewing when Edane ran in and then everything came down on us." She looked up at the housekeeper and held out her arm. "I'm not lying. Please, go ahead and check me."

Rosealise smiled at her. "You're quite resourceful, my dear girl, but not even you could make part of a castle fall on your head."

"Aye," her husband said. "'Tis an ancient place. Doubtless the stone crumbled on its own."

Nellie recognized the look they gave each other, and knew that now she was the one being lied to.

Chapter Nineteen

⚜

WITH THE REMNANT stonework still at risk of falling, Edane helped his brothers block off the passage and shore up the remaining wall to keep the rubble from spilling into the kitchens. The work also helped curbed some of the rage roiling inside him.

Nellie had nearly been burned and then crushed to death, and he would not rest until he knew why.

Once the area had been made safe, Domnall sent Broden to watch over Nellie and Rosealise, and signaled for the rest of the hunters to follow him out of the stronghold to the greenhouse, where Jenna was waiting.

There he paused until Edane invoked the silencing spell, and then draped his tartan across the inside panels so they could not be seen.

As Mael and Kiaran did the same to the sides of the structure, Edane attended to blocking the back panels. The time for clever subterfuge had ended.

The chieftain regarded his wife. "Tell us what you ken."

"I looked over the damage inside and out," Jenna said, and wiped some dirt from her chin with the back of her hand. "Nothing inside from the pantry or the exterior of the stronghold caused the collapse. Kiaran and I did a little digging at the foundation, but we didn't find any tunnels under them, either. I need to go through them to be sure."

"You dinnae need again burn off your hair," Domnall told her sternly. "'Twas rot, then."

"My ass it was." His wife's eyes flashed with ire. "I personally inspected that room, multiple times. I looked again before we put Nellie in there, just to be sure there wasn't a way for her to get out. Last night those walls were solid and sound. Someone did this today."

Kiaran looked skeptical. "If 'tis as you say, and only the wench occupied the chamber, then–"

"Nellie would have died, had I no' shielded her." Edane felt Mael's big hand on his shoulder, and reined in his temper. "Why would she go back to the pantry to sew if she'd set the walls to fall?"

"Boys, let's remember who's the architect here. I have a working theory." Jenna reached into her skirt pocket and pulled out a wedge-shaped fragment of stone. "This is a piece of a boss, what you guys call a keystone. I noticed that it and several other large ashlar stones have fresh cracks in them."

"Aye, lass, for they're old, and fell with great force," Mael pointed out.

"Yeah, that's what it looks like." She tossed the stone up and down in her hand. "Funny how all the stones appeared intact yesterday, but decided to shatter today. To drop the walls, at least a dozen of them in the perfect positions broke at the exact same time. I didn't feel an earthquake, did any of you?"

"'Twasnae by chance," Kiaran said, looking ready to launch into another condemnation of Nellie. Then he met Edane's furious gaze and shook his head.

"Easy, lads," the seneschal said. "Let our lady have her say."

"I can tell you the one person who didn't do this: Nellie," Jenna told the falconer. "There's no way she could have chosen the correct stones to crack. She also didn't have any tools or the strength to do it. If she had, we would have heard her hammering away. This was done by someone powerful, silent, and who knows how to build a castle. Sound like anyone she's described lately?"

The falconer glanced at the chieftain. "More lies, likely. Your lady feels pity for the lass. I dinnae."

"You know, Kiaran, if I had magical powers or a stealth jackhammer, *I* could have done it," Jenna told him. "Want to point the finger at me now? No? Then look at this."

She went to Edane's planting bench, where she stacked some small clay seedling pots in two vertical piles and poured dirt in between them.

"Most of Dun Chaill's structure was made of two stone walls with gravel and dirt filling the space between them, like so." Jenna tamped down and molded the dirt until it joined the two stacks. "That's Medieval Scottish Castle Wall Building 101. Take notes because there'll be a pop quiz later."

Edane saw the chieftain and Mael casually shift so that they stood between him and the falconer. Then he glanced down and saw he'd wrapped his fist around the hilt of his dagger. He released the blade and took in a calming breath.

"Imagine this is one of the pantry walls. Take away a stone here and there." Jenna removed two of the pots. "It holds. It would if you cracked most of the other stones. But damage a boss or a stone that supports the weight load?" She tugged at a pot at the bottom of the stack, and soil began to crumble away. "The weights begin to shift. The stones dependent on that support then redistribute their weight, and the structure weakens even more. Ultimately it creates a cascading failure."

"You're certain of this?" Kiaran asked.

"Jenna nearly died in a building collapse in her time," Domnall reminded him. "The Sluath took her from the rubble as she lay dying."

The falconer had the grace to look sheepish. "I didnae think on that. Forgive me, my lady."

"Uh-huh. So, let's see what happens with a little more damage here and there." Jenna tugged at a number of the pots. That made the others above it fall, and the dirt spilled over the top of them. A moment later the opposite stack teetered and fell into a heap. "Any questions?"

Her husband studied the mess. "How can you be sure the stones didnae simply crack from ruination?"

"You mean, aside from the fact that I would have noticed, and I would never have let you put Nellie next to unsafe walls?" She picked up the keystone and turned it on its side. "See the green stain on the inside of this cracked edge? I think it's from fresh moss being stuffed inside and over it. I saw more stains like that on other stones."

"Placed to hide the tampering," Edane

said, remembering what he'd seen in the Great Hall. "Chieftain, 'twas the watcher's doing."

As he told them of what he had observed about the fire trap just before the collapse, Kiaran kept silent. Domnall's expression grew harsher, and Jenna rubbed her brow. Mael went several times to tug aside an edge of a tartan to look out at the stronghold. Edane knew he was worried about his wife. All he wanted to do was fetch Nellie and take her far from Dun Chaill.

But if we go beyond the spell boundary, the Sluath shall find us.

"So, the watcher's back," Jenna said, and the men nodded. "How do we deal with this jerk?"

"We hunt." The chieftain put his arm around her shoulders. "We shall begin searching anew, using the grid map my lady drew for us of the stronghold. Edane, we'll need your magic now."

He nodded. "The ward stones I used before remain in place. I've but to activate them to trace any movements no' our own through the keepe."

"See it done tonight." Domnall regarded

the other men. "Carry your weapons and remain on your mettle at all times. We'll set a watch in the keepe day and night. Kiaran, send your kestrels to patrol the towers and passages. Jenna, you and I shall return to the pantry, and look for any trace the watcher left behind there that may give away his hiding place. Mael, you shall guard our other ladies–"

"No," Edane said. "He's tried twice to end Nellie. I brought the lass here, and 'tis my duty to protect her. I'll no' have her sleep in the stronghold again."

The chieftain hesitated before he nodded. "Where shall you take her, then, Brother? No' the forest. 'Tis too open."

"We'll sleep in the one place I can make safe for her." Edane gestured around them. "Here, in the greenhouse."

※

ONCE ROSEALISE HAD finished CLEANING and bandaging the last of Nellie's cuts, she took her into the kitchens and made a soothing brew for her. The flapper behaved calmly, but every sound made her gaze dart and her body tense. Broden also picked up on her nervousness, and came to sit and speak with her about the dairy and the cows.

Listening to them made Rosealise wonder again about Nellie's past. For a thoroughly carefree, unskilled young lady, she had a startling knowledge of the dairy. She also showed no distaste over caring for the animals when Broden proposed they together examine the cattle for hoof injuries. Growing up in the country, the housekeeper had helped her father tend to their family's two milk cows, which had involved dirty and often unpleasant work. Since Nellie had insisted her appearance was of the utmost personal importance, her easiness with livestock work seemed quite out of place.

"I'd have Kiaran forge the knives for cutting back the hooves," Broden said. "Yet I've never done such work."

"I can draw the one that my– Ow." Nellie winced and rubbed her temple. "I can draw one for him."

Adding several dollops of honey to the herbal tisane, Rosealise brought the mug to the flapper, who warmed her hands against the sides. "Edane has made a tincture of willow bark that may ease your headache, Miss Quinn."

"Or I can stop trying to remember how I know so much about cows." She took a sip of the brew and grimaced. "Jeepers, this is super sweet."

"Yes, but that's good for settling nerves, and I fear yours are as bruised as the rest of you," Rosealise assured her as she brought another mug for the trapper. "Would you like honey in yours, my dear sir?"

"Thank you no, my lady." Broden's smile didn't quite reach his eyes, which shifted as he scanned the room. Approaching footsteps put him on his feet, his sword in hand. He relaxed only as he saw Edane and the others come in from the outside. "'Tis well?"

"Aye." The archer came to Nellie, while Rosealise went to greet her husband.

"Edane shall stay with the lass in the greenhouse tonight," Mael said as the pair left the kitchens. "They shall fetch the bedding while I go to make it ready. Jenna and Domnall shall have another look at the pantry. Broden's for patrol and then first watch." The falconer passed them with a small incline of his head and headed to the kitchens. "Stay with Kiaran until I return." Mael embraced her and whispered, "The watcher's returned, my love. 'Twas his doing."

A surge of dread added to Rosealise's burgeoning worry, but now was not the time for hysterics. She nodded and kissed her husband before she went to make up more calming brew. As she measured out the herbs, she saw the falconer station himself to look out through the garden window.

"Would you care for a brew?" she asked him. "I'll have more ready very soon."

"No, my lady." He came over to join her. "You neednae worry the chieftain shall ask you to use your power on the wench again. Jenna reckons she couldnae have caused the collapse."

That Nellie was the source of his displeasure didn't surprise her. "Don't you agree?"

"'Twasnae work she could manage alone," Kiaran said, his tone as chilly as his dark eyes, "but another at her bidding might have."

Clearly the man's grudge against the flapper had grown beyond reason, and the injustice of blaming the girl did not sit well with Rosealise at all.

"When do you imagine Miss Quinn arranged such villainous work with our enemies?" she asked in her sweetest voice. "When she was running away from you last night into that tunnel of fire? Or was it after the chieftain had her imprisoned in the pantry? Perhaps Broden turned away for a moment when they were milking the cows. Doubtless she had some secret signal to instruct the Sluath to drop the walls on her head."

The falconer glowered at her. "'Tis no' a jest, my lady. You yourself compelled her to admit she's a thieving liar."

"Yes, I did, and I hope in time she will forgive me for that." Rosealise prided herself on being a non-violent soul, which was the only reason she didn't toss her brew in his face. "I must say, what terror will drive someone to do is quite astonishing." She saw his eyes narrow and knew instinctively that she had hit on what needled him so greatly. "Is your dislike of Nellie fueled by a close acquaintance with the same sort of desperation, sir?"

Instantly his expression blanked. "I dinnae ken your meaning, my lady." He returned to his stance by the window, his shoulders stiff now.

"Oh, yes, you do," she muttered under her breath.

A moment later Jenna and Domnall came in, both disheveled and dusty. The chieftain beckoned to the falconer, leading him outside.

Rosealise brought the architect a damp cloth to wipe her hands and face, and smelled singed hair. "You burned yourself walking through the walls again?"

"I wanted to be sure it wasn't a structural failure." Jenna touched her short bob and grimaced. "I stopped as soon as my hair started to get hot. Then I went to show Domnall the stones that looked as if they'd been tampered with, but they were all gone."

Chapter Twenty

NELLIE DIDN'T OBJECT when Edane told her she would be spending the rest of the night in the greenhouse. She figured with the pantry destroyed they'd need a new place to keep her. Being anywhere but inside the castle seemed fine to her. If need be, she'd sleep with the cows out in the pasture.

"'Twillnae be as warm as the keepe," Edane said as he led her into the small outbuilding, in which some candles provided a little light. "But Mael brought many window coverings."

Little plants sprouted from dozens of clay pots, and made the air smell like an herb garden. Hand tools hung from a carved rack above a wooden table lined with more pots. She saw the wood sorrel they'd gathered, now tidily planted in the tiniest containers.

Nellie bent down and lifted one corner of the wool that covered the mound on the dirt floor, and saw some old sacking atop a pile of clean fleeces. More blankets sat stacked next to the makeshift bed.

"Looks real cozy." The last thing she wanted to do was sleep, so she leaned against the table and glanced at the only door. "Is Broden going to barricade me inside, or do you plan to tie me to something?"

"You're not our prisoner, my lady. 'Tis only that you're safer kept here with us." When she arched her brows, he sighed. "With me, then. I'll stay the night with you, and we can talk."

"You don't have to guard me," Nellie assured him. "I've learned my lesson. I won't run away again."

But if a chance to get away from Dun Chaill came along, she certainly wouldn't resist it. She wanted to live.

"'Tisnae what I mean." Edane took hold of her hand. "We need to speak truth now, you and I. Give me a moment to make us safe."

He went to secure the door with a bolt bar, and then spread out his hands. Dark blue light glowed briefly on his marked arm as he murmured under his breath.

"What was that?" Nellie asked once he fell silent.

"I cast a warding spell to protect us. If anything comes near while we sleep, 'twill awaken me." He turned to face her. "I didnae tell you that I'm shaman-trained to use magic. Mayhap the chieftain should imprison me."

"Probably not." She rubbed the tingling marks on the back of her neck. "Anything else I ought to know?"

Edane grimaced. "Aye."

As he told her about the watcher, the cold part of her saw a perfect opportunity coming together. Edane's anger and guilt over what had happened to her could easily be turned into what she wanted. Showing the right amount of fear and pain could convince him to take her away until the clan figured out who the watcher was, and why he was trying to hurt her. The scheme seemed like the smart thing to do. The only problem was that Edane had saved her life twice. He deserved better than to be used again.

"So, you've got someone hiding in the castle who doesn't like me. Guess Kiaran will make a new friend." She eased down on the blanket and leaned back against the table's leg, patting the space beside her. "Now come here and keep me warm, fella."

"'Tis something more you should ken." He looked even more uncomfortable now. "Broden told me what he meant to offer you this morning, so I might ken your true regard for me. I watched from the loft as he did. For that I reckon the chieftain would punish me."

So Broden and I really are the same, Nellie thought, and chuckled. Only the sound came out wrong, and then the candlelight grew blurry as the iciness inside her started to crack.

"Forgive me, my lady," Edane said, kneeling down in front of her.

She turned her head and stared at a big plant with stalky purple flowers. It smelled heavenly, like Rosealise's brews.

Nellie didn't hate the guys for scamming her, only that Edane thought he had to. There wasn't a bit of him that was cold or mean or selfish. She loved how soft and gentle his voice felt, as if he were hugging her with every word. He looked at her as if she were the same, even when he knew she wasn't. She loved his kindness, and his long, beautiful hands, and the endless sky in his eyes. It didn't matter than she couldn't remember her past anymore. She knew she'd never met any guy like him.

That was why she couldn't hold onto the cold part of herself.

I love him and it's making me fall apart.

As Edane moved to sit beside her, Nellie drew up her knees and rested her brow against them, trying to keep the tears back. They came anyway, along with huge, wrenching sobs that tore out of her chest.

Strong hands draped her with a tartan, and then Edane curled an arm around her shoulders. He didn't say a word, but simply held onto her. When she finally got hold of herself and sat up again, he used an edge of the plaid to dry her face.

"Better now?" When she nodded, he said, "I've given you the truth I held back, and I'm sorry it took so long. Will you now tell me what plagues you still? 'Tis a memory from your past?"

"Something did come back to me," Nellie said, glad for the suggestion. "When we were doing the Charleston with the clan last night, I remembered another place. People from my time were dancing there. A scary-looking guy walked past me, and said I looked swanky. It gave me the creeps."

His hand touched her cheek. "That didnae make you cry."

Telling him that she'd fallen in love with him served no purpose. He must have heard what she'd told Broden in the barn. "It's been a long day. Again."

"Then I shall show one of my secrets." He reached into his tunic, and took out a large wool pouch, which he placed in her hands.

Nellie untied it, and turned it over her palm. A long strand of round white beads slithered into her hand, cool and perfect. The candlelight made the necklace glow with a faint golden luster.

"Are these real pearls?"

Edane nodded. "I've been collecting them

since we escaped the Sluath. I drilled the holes in each, and strung them on fine silk. I hid the work from my brothers so they wouldnae ken. I didnae reckon why I made the necklace, until I found you."

"What did I do?" she said, puzzled.

"You came to me at last." He put the strand over her head, tugging it down around her throat. "'Twas waiting for you, my lady. Like me, all of my life."

Chapter Twenty-One

MOONLIGHT FELL ON Cul's scowling face like a splash of cold water, carving from his distorted visage a mask of sharp lines and lumpy curves. He sniffed the night air, catching a trace of Pritani magic. He would have attributed it to the Mag Raith's archer, who had considerable skill as a shaman, but this seeking spell had been invoked from a greater distance. He had refined Dun Chaill's boundary to allow such castings to make their way to him, but not to reflect anything back.

So, it seemed someone was looking for something.

Magic descended on the garden maze, spangling the hedges before swirling around

Cul. As it found him, he lifted his hands to capture it and contain it with his own power. He sifted through the threads of the enchantment and found it had been cast by Galan Aedth. It had considerable power, thanks to the prince's gift to the druid, but not enough to trouble Cul. The spell had not been cast to hunt the Mag Raith, however, but sought a very different kind of immortal.

Has the prince at last thought of something beyond his own pleasures, and bid his pet druid to look for his long-lost kin?

Cul brought his hands together and shattered the spell, absorbing its power as he considered what that would mean for his plans.

Since emerging from the crumbled tower, evading the keen eyes of the Mag Raith and the falconer's kestrels required Cul to be particularly cunning. He cast over himself a body ward that concealed his shape and movements wherever he went after the sun set. It cloaked him in such convincing darkness that he appeared nothing more than a flat shadow.

It had also allowed him to follow Nellie out of the stronghold when she attempted her escape. When she'd tried to flee from the Mag Raith, he'd quickly opened one of the new fire traps he'd created from his old access passages, and she'd hurried into it. The trap should have roasted her alive, but the clan had banded together to save her.

He would have strangled her as she slept in the pantry that night, but the trapper had blocked the only access to it with immense stones. So Cul had to resort to more drastic measures to insure her demise. When he heard the collapse of the pantry walls, he emerged from the tunnels and waited in the passage as the clan hurried in, only to see Nellie carried out by the archer, both battered and bloody but still alive.

It had astounded him to see her in Edane's arms. He'd never known a mortal female to have such remarkable luck. Not even Dun Chaill could kill her.

Knowing Nellie could read what he had done from the stones, Cul hastily removed every one he had bespelled, dragging pieces down into his access tunnel before sealing it behind him.

Destroying part of his castle to be rid of

the touch-reader had been a costly risk, but one he'd been convinced would serve. Yet once he'd used his listening post to eavesdrop on the clan's conversations, he knew his scheme had only alerted the Mag Raith to his presence again. Furious that he had exposed himself by attempting the opposite, Cul had limped through the tunnels and climbed up through the maze entry.

Finding the druid's seeking spell had cooled much of his temper, but he had to attend to the touch-reader now before she and her nuisance powers drove him mad.

He flung a surge of his magic at a side section of thorny hedges, which parted enough for him to look through to the surrounding pathways. From there he watched as Edane mag Raith led Nellie from the stronghold into the greenhouse. A few moments later he saw the shimmer of magic envelope the outbuilding.

The archer seeks to protect her from further harm.

Cul could easily dissolve the ward with his own, superior magic. He'd wait until they slept, slip inside, and kill them both. The clan would be none the wiser until the morning.

The sound of footsteps made him turn to see one of his iron warriors approaching. He'd sent a dozen out to patrol the boundary and keep watch for the Sluath or any intruders. They would return only if they had news to impart. He redirected his sentinel to walk to the maze, where he led him down into his tunnels. Once there he took the warrior into his spell chamber, where he lifted the enchantment that controlled him just enough for the man to speak.

"What do you bring me?" Cul demanded.

In a flinty voice the warrior said, "The druid Aedth came to the glen. He didnae approach the boundary. He rode to the old Pritani settlement. He removed bones from a grave. He took them with him and rode toward the Sluath village."

"Where was the grave located?" As the sentinel described the site, Cul knew where Galan had gone, but not why. "Did the druid do anything more while at the grave?"

"Aye," the warrior said. "He cried out a word: Fiana."

The name echoed in Cul's head, leaping through the long centuries of his exile in Dun

Chaill to the time of his enslavement in the underworld. There, bound by such chains that nothing could break, he had endured unending torments. His suffering might have ended him but for the king's lust for an heir deemed worthy of his bloodline.

Cul had seen Prince Iolar born, the last of the Sluath begat by flesh. Stunningly beautiful in his white and gold glory, the young demon had more than fulfilled his sire's requirements. He had gone on to acquire power and allies among the other demons, all with alarming ease. Once he had swayed most of the Sluath to pledge their loyalty to him, Iolar had murdered his sire and seized the throne.

Baleful delight spread through Cul as he realized how he could use the druid. He had no doubt now that Galan Aedth desired to resurrect the dead Pritani female whose bones he had stolen from the grave. That explained the seeking spell he'd cast. Perhaps he would do anything to see her restored to life.

Just as Cul would, so the druid might know the truth of his dreams.

Collecting himself, Cul restored the

enchantment and grinned at the sentinel's flat metallic eyes staring back at him.

"Return to the glen, and continue your watch."

The iron warrior left as silently as he had arrived.

Cul knew his preoccupation with killing Nellie Quinn had caused him to lose sight of the greater prey. Indeed, he'd seen her death as the means with which to protect himself and Dun Chaill. Laughter burst from him, harsh and gloating. Nellie Quinn's outrageous luck still held. She would serve him better alive than dead, for now.

Chapter Twenty-Two

KIARAN WALKED ALONG the curtain wall, stopping when he found the spot where the arch leading into the fire trap had appeared. The weathered stones felt solid and unyielding under his hand, as if they'd stood there for centuries. Edane had claimed the watcher responsible for setting the trap, and that Nellie had only triggered it to open with her touch. Turning over every detail of what had occurred in his thoughts had not provided anything to the contrary. He also remembered how the flapper had tried to make him leave the passage just before they had become trapped.

Dive and her mate circled over his head,

their sharp eyes showing him his own rigid back and clenched fists.

"You'll find no trace of the portal," Broden's grating voice said. "Earlier Edane all but plied a sledge to that wall, but it didnae again appear. Or would you say the wench bewitched his senses?"

"'Tis no guessing what she may do." He stepped back from the wall as the trapper stopped beside him. "I thought you've the watch tonight."

"Aye, but the chieftain bid me first patrol the outer walls." Broden gestured to the trail surrounding the stronghold. "Walk with me."

Kiaran fell into step beside him, braced for yet another tongue-lashing for speaking against Nellie. When the trapper remained silent, he grew even more annoyed.

"Dinnae you wish to persuade me to see Mistress Quinn's innocence? Such a harmless and sweet lass, and I the unfeeling brute for accusing her."

Broden halted and regarded him for a long moment. "I tried to seduce her in the barn this morning. She refused me, out of love for

Edane. Then she told me how she felt, being in Dun Chaill."

Kiaran listened to him recount Nellie's words, and in them heard a truth he knew only too well. When the trapper finished, he finally had to admit defeat.

"She's no' a spy, then."

"No more than I, Brother." Broden continued on the path. "Now 'tis time for you to confess what you've long concealed from us."

Kiaran nearly tripped over his own feet. "What?"

"You do naught without cause. I'll wager your ire toward the lass came from your distrust of Galan." At Kiaran's quick look he nodded. "Aye, I saw how you watched him from the moment he entered the ash grove after our escape, to spin his tales."

"I didnae care for the facking *dru-wid*." He moved his shoulders. "Neither did Domnall."

"Why?" The trapper halted outside the granary where Kiaran slept. "He provided us with haven and purpose. You wouldnae cross him or question his orders. Indeed, 'twas ever your habit to avoid the man. I'll wager if no' for the rest of us, you'd have left the enchanted forest long before we found Jenna."

"I kept my oath to protect the Moss Dapple," he said flatly. "In that I honored the chieftain's wishes."

"Now you lie to me." Broden stepped in front of him as he reached for the door latch. "You sensed something amiss with the bastart, didnae you?"

"'Tis of no consequence now. He's shown himself our enemy." He took hold of the latch. "Fair night, Brother."

A fist rammed against the door, slamming it shut. "You saw through Galan's lies from the very beginning, and yet never uttered a word to any of us. Such honor, Kiaran."

"I but suspected." He rubbed his brow, and then dropped his hand to meet the trapper's hard gaze. "All the *dru-wid* said obliged us to him, and destroyed any reason we'd have for leaving. As the centuries passed his interest in our immortality and our powers swelled, and in the last century reeked of covetousness. I did wish to tell you, but 'twasnae my place to gainsay Domnall."

"You might have told him," Broden said.

Kiaran shrugged. "I'm no' Mag Raith by blood. You and I arenae Mael or Edane. We're outsiders, tolerated for our skills."

"So you mean now to redeem yourself for your silence." Broden pointed beyond him toward the greenhouse. "'Tis why you've tried to turn the clan against Nellie. You ken you should have done so before, with Galan. Your anger and disgust with him have poisoned you against the lass."

"No, Brother." Kiaran thought of the day he had first stumbled into the Mag Raith's settlement, filthy and starving, the rags of his garments crusted with dark Pritani blood. "'Twas a betrayal long before that."

Chapter Twenty-Three

❦

THE PEARLS FELL down to Nellie's waist, and stroking her fingers along them sent flashes of Edane's hands creating the necklace through her mind. Yet when his fingers covered hers, all she could see was him beside her, the sky in his eyes bright with pleasure, as if he'd been given the gift.

She couldn't let him do this. "Did you forget that the demons gave you to me as a slave?"

"Aye." Edane stroked the necklace with her fingers and his.

"Don't be a wise guy." Why wasn't he still angry with her? As he bent his head down, she gripped his tattooed arm, and the ink on the back of her neck grew hot. "This is a big mistake, fella. You don't want a no-good floozy like me."

"You're my *peyrl*," he murmured, his mouth hovering over hers. "'Tis naught I want but you."

Some of the candles flickered out, pulling the shadows around them. Nellie gave up and met him the rest of the way, her lips trembling against his, her fingers curling over the glyphs on his skin. She'd make this her thank-you for all the lovely things he'd said. When it ended, she'd say she felt worn out and needed to sleep. He would curl up with her, and hold her through the dark hours. Having him wrapped around her would be enough.

She just had to stop kissing him now.

Only his mouth on hers felt too good, and where his hands stroked her back a delicious warmth spread. He groaned against her lips, the hungry sound humming through her. She let it go on, parting her lips for his tongue, drinking in the taste of his desire. He wanted her so badly that she could feel how much. Every corded muscle in his body coiled, and his skin grew hot where she touched him. Her breasts ached against his hard chest, her nipples pebbling, eager for his touch. Between her thighs everything became full and drenched and throbbed madly, as low sounds spilled from her mouth to his.

But it wasn't her that ended the kiss. Edane pulled back and cradled her face in his hands. "You're too hurt for more, lass."

"That what you think?"

Nellie couldn't feel a single ache from her cuts and bruises as she stood, and tugged down the too-large bodice to her waist before dropping Rosealise's dress to her boots. Stepping out of both, she straightened and stood naked but for a few bandages and his pearls.

"Not bleeding. Nothing hurts at all." She turned around slowly and fanned herself with her hand. "But I do feel kinda hot."

Edane looked up at her, a sweet torment in his eyes. "You neednae do this tonight, lass."

"That's the thing." She straddled his legs and reached for the bottom of his tunic. "We could have died today. We should do this for us." She hesitated. "But if you don't want to–"

He used her hands to tug off his tunic.

Baring his chest led to stroking the hard walls of lean muscle cording it, which then she had to kiss. The scent of him engulfed her, so good she never wanted anything but him as her breath. She felt him rub his hand over her curls, and twined her fingers in his long scarlet mane, drawing the bright strands over her face. Through that veil everything looked as if it were webbed by golden spiders spinning tangerine silks.

He shifted, easing her down to lay beside him on the wool blanket. "You should ken that as immortals we cannae sire bairns, my lady."

"You mean make babies?" As he nodded Nellie felt a wrenching sadness, not just for him but for all the men. Then she realized he was reassuring her that she wouldn't end up pregnant from this. Then she knew what to say. "Probably for the best. Kiaran would say that I stole the kid and hid him in my belly."

That startled a laugh out of him. "I wager he would."

Nellie grinned and slipped her hands around his waist, pulling him close before she tugged at his laces. "Time to let me see what you look like naked, fella."

He reached back to help her, and then rolled away to remove his boots before he stripped off his trousers.

Every long, strong inch of him made Nellie's fingers itch to touch him, but she could have just looked at him for the rest of the night, too. He didn't have the bulging muscular bulk of the other men, but instead looked lean and tough, like his bows. Would he make love like his arrows flew, straight and sure? Scarlet curls adorned the base of his long, erect cock, which stood up straight against his belly.

Could she take all of him? Nellie wondered as she reached out to stroke the hard shaft. Yet the moment she touched him she felt the hot, wet softness between her thighs tighten with anticipation, not fear. Then she thought of the erotic end of the memory they'd shared, and smiled to herself. Maybe he'd been her slave once, but now she wanted to be his, and she knew exactly where she wanted him inside her.

"Do I please you?" he asked, as if he were actually worried about it.

She brushed her lips against his. "Let me take a closer look."

The pearls pooled on his thighs as she leaned closer, pressing her lips to his straining crown. He felt like iron but tasted like his scent, and she had to have more. She caressed him with her tongue, licking his cockhead like a delicious sweet, the throbbing heat of him luscious. When she parted her lips and bathed him with her breath he jerked and then let out a deep groan as she took him into her mouth.

"Oh, lass." Edane's hand shook as he stroked the curls back from her cheeks. "'Tis too much."

She would have explained why it wasn't, but licking and sucking him absorbed Nellie entirely. The intimate act brought from the shadows in her mind a sense of having done so many times. She wished she could remember, just for him, for in the underworld she must have known ways to give him the most pleasure.

On and on Nellie loved him, lavishing all the sensual hunger she had on his hard cock. He shook and swore softly as she discovered how to tilt her head to take him deeper. She never wanted it to end, for in this way she had him as no one else ever would. This was theirs, only theirs, and no one could be part of it but them. As selfish as she was, she'd never felt delighted to give instead of take, except for this.

"I'll soon spend." His thigh muscles tensed as his shaft swelled between her tugging lips. "Nellie."

She wanted that part of him, too, and held on and took him as deeply as she could. His hands fisted in her hair and his cock pulsed and jerked in her mouth. She swallowed the jets of seed that came from him, thick and silken, and wallowed in the deep sounds he made with each one. At last it ended, and when she let him escape her lips, she kissed the head of his shaft one more time.

Falling on the fleeces with him made her chuckle a little. She felt so strange, almost as if some terrible weight had been lifted off her chest. As Edane gathered her against him she wondered if she might take them both floating up to the thatched roof.

"I'd vow I've never felt such pleasure, my lady," he murmured as he studied her face. He ran his thumb along the swollen curves of her lips. "Yet I believe I have. 'Twas how you meant to love me in the vision."

She kissed his hand. "I'm glad you like it, because it's my new favorite thing to do with you."

"Ah, but I've no' had a chance to offer the same." He ran his hand from her shoulder to her hip. "I want to bring you to bliss with my mouth, and my hands, and my cock. I'll fill your nights with so many joys you'll never wish to leave my bed."

Nellie felt the lightness recede, and something else took its place. It felt like water, dark and cold, just a thin trickle that ran down from the back of her neck to follow the length of her necklace. The sluggish chill of it made her shiver.

"I'll warm you now," Edane said, pulling her closer.

"Love me." The words popped out of her mouth before she could stop them, and she saw the answering pleasure in his eyes. "I mean, yes, please, do anything and everything you want. I want all of you."

He rolled over her, bracing his long body

on his elbows as if he thought he weighed too much. She laughed and pulled him down, relishing the press of his hard chest on her breasts, and the sinuous twine of his legs with hers.

"I'm not going to break," she promised, stretching her arms over her head. "Have all the fun you want, fella."

"I hardly ken where to begin."

Edane's gaze shifted over her face before he kissed her, his mouth firm and hungry. The heat of his breath made her feel a little drunk, and then he stroked her tongue with his. The way he kissed her stirred everything inside her back to full, aching need again. She arched under him, lifting her hips so she could rub herself against his swelling erection.

"My lady," he muttered against her lips, and then followed the line of her throat down to her breasts.

Oh, why had she told him to do whatever he wanted? Nellie looked down to watch him kiss her nipples, and then he was sucking and licking and driving her out of her skull. He did things to her with his mouth that made her shake, and the only breathing she could do was in tight, frantic gasps. When he would have continued down to kiss her belly, she gave into her own desires and tugged at him.

"I take it back," she told him as he smiled at her. "I need one thing, right now, and it's not your mouth. Next time, anything and everything, I swear."

Edane gathered her up with one arm and reached between them with another. He brought his cock between her thighs so gently and carefully she groaned, and then notched himself against her. She'd grown so wet he sank into her softness, his shaft so smooth that it glided into her like someone had wrapped it in satin.

"Lass." His jaw tightened as he tried to slow his penetration. "You feel…as a maiden."

He probably meant virgin. Nellie didn't remember if she was, knew it was unlikely, and frankly didn't care.

"Okay. I'll find a shotgun and make you marry me. Tomorrow. Or maybe the next day." She rolled her hips under his. "Please, please, please."

Edane got that message, and gave her a long, delicious thrust. No pain came with it, just slow, silky satisfaction. He stroked out and in, filling her deep, his shaft so hard now she felt herself melting around him. Oh, but it was so good, so perfect. He felt so long inside her she wondered if she had taken him all, and then found out she hadn't when he plowed even deeper.

She tried to kiss whatever her lips could touch, his neck and chin and mouth, and then pressed her mouth to his shoulder as he began pumping into her. The muffled sounds of her whimpering seemed to unleash some beast in him, for he gripped her hips and stroked into her faster.

Nellie held on as long as she could, her nails dragging down his arms as he fucked her, but the bliss took her over and tore at her until all she could do was surrender. The hot rush of pleasure grew tight and then blasted out, flinging the ecstasy he'd promised into every part of her body. Nothing could be this enthralling and destroying. She might just die on the spot.

Edane held her through the shaking, and then thrust twice more before it was his turn. He spilled this time, filling her with such fountaining warmth Nellie shuddered with delight. Then they lay together, trembling now and then as their bodies cooled. At some point she realized she was still wearing his pearls, and lifted her fingers to touch the strand.

Now you've gone and done it.

Nellie hated that coldness inside her. She never wanted to hear from it again. She was with a guy who made her feel happy and satisfied and definitely not a virgin. Didn't she deserve that, after all she'd been through? Demons and monsters and falling walls? Couldn't she just have this?

"You must tell me of shotguns," Edane said as he propped himself up and looked down at her. "Why do they make men marry?"

"Not tonight, fella," Nellie said, her eyelids fluttered as she tried to keep them open. The pearls seemed heavier now, almost dragging at her neck, but she was too tired to remove them. "I'm sorry, but I'm really beat. Let's get some sleep."

"Aye, if 'tis your wish." Edane sounded puzzled, but pulled her close and covered them with the blanket. "You never said if I pleased you, my lady."

"You're the bee's knees," Nellie murmured, cuddling against him as she closed her eyes.

Chapter Twenty-Four

⚜

IN EDANE'S ARMS Nellie fell into a cold river of memories. They swept her along until she found herself in New York City, and the speakeasy where she'd spent her last night as a flapper. The joint, called The Doll's Drum, had been Nellie's last stop on her long, ugly journey.

Like all the underground clubs in Manhattan it looked like a ramshackle version of heaven or hell. Which one depended on how drunk the patrons got.

On this night smoke from countless cigarettes rose like thin ghosts toward the punched tin ceiling, which trapped it in a diaphanous, malodorous cloud. Sequined dresses and painted lips flashed in the light from the big bulbs strung like crepe overhead. Trails of French perfume followed the flappers tottering back and forth to tables to gossip with friends or flirt with their men. Now and then an argument would break out, drawing one of the big goons posted by the club's walls and doors.

A quiet word from one of them usually shut up the loudmouths. If it didn't, they walked them back to a private room no one ever had to visit twice.

Sipping a glass containing water with only a splash of whiskey, Nellie leaned back against the bar to take in the show. The glaring stage lights made her new dress glitter like a column of gilded ice. Her clothes and the long pearl necklace she wore kept the plugs from thinking her a pro skirt. Nellie had studied film actresses Colleen Moore and Louise Brooks as she'd polished and perfected the image of a vibrant, fun-loving flapper.

You can't just look the part, Cap had warned her. *You have to make yourself a good-time girl.*

Nellie had and, over time, slipping into her part had become effortless. Tonight she'd clipped some fresh tiger lilies to her three-tiered head band, which kept her fringe slanted saucily over her kohl-rimmed eyes. Her silver t-strap shoes had the highest heels she could walk in, which helped show off her thin, svelte figure. She smelled of the lilies and the hooch she'd dabbed behind her ears and on her lips to complete her ritzy masquerade.

More like a chippy, ya big sap. Michael Patrick Quinn's young, freckled face scowled at her from the corner of her mind where she'd tucked his memory. *You've done enough to find the guy. Cap will do the rest. Get out of here. It's not too late.*

Even dead her little brother could still needle her. *Not just yet, Mickie. Got to send over the whole bunch.*

Onstage the band belted out the Charleston Strut, luring every tipsy dish who could nab a partner for a hoof on the floor. Nellie tapped her toes to the song as she giggled at the dancers. None of them would guess how much she hated the tune. She sometimes dreamed of the banjos strumming over her grave. The couples always looked feverish, almost frantic to have fun, as if someone might shoot them if they didn't.

These days most of the rubes looked too

young to her, but after living this way for so long she felt as old and frayed as her mother's milking apron.

And whose fault is that? Mickie demanded.

Nellie had no problem accepting the blame for what she'd done to land in this spot. If she didn't get what she wanted tonight, she knew she'd have to work on Jackie himself. Everyone knew she'd run around with plenty of trouble boys. A few more lies spilled into his ear would wind him up nice and tight. To get enough time alone to do that, she'd probably have to get cozy with him.

Could she make whoopee with the murdering big shot? So far that was the one thing she hadn't done. The thought of it made Nellie feel as if her heart had turned to stone, and what little good left in her was about to be crushed under its weight.

No way to wash that off, Mickie whispered inside her ear. *You let that snake between your knees and you'll never feel clean again.*

If she had to bed the boss to bring down him and his thugs, she'd damn well do it. Chasing Jackie down had gotten her too dirty to ever be that girl from the family farm again.

She'd never go back to the country, not after being soaked in the muck of her own making. All that mattered was making good on what she'd promised herself. It was the only way it would be worth what it had cost her.

"Say, looking swank tonight, Baby," a gravelly voice said as a thin shadow stretched over her face.

Nellie gave Dapper a pout and a peek through her eyelashes as thanks, but the tall, skeletal man passed her by without missing a step. It felt like being spared a nightmare and missing a jackpot. Between the pricey black bowler and the over-waxed mustache, the killer's muddy eyes remained as dead as corpse coins. Jackie Facelli's number one hatchet man always complimented her when he came into the club, in the same, routine way he murdered whoever the boss wanted chilled, or whoever got in his way.

Some he'd killed for no reason at all.

Out of the corner of her eye Nellie watched Dapper head straight for the two guns standing at the other end of the bar. He took off his hat and dropped it on the bar while he spoke to them, and then the three disappeared into the manager's office. Very slowly, still watching the dancers, Nellie wandered down to the hat. Bracing herself, she touched the rim and opened herself up.

Everything Dapper had done earlier that night came through her, replaying inside her head like a movie. Instead of music, she heard sounds and voices, like the talkies everyone said Hollywood would soon be making.

Dapper had first touched the bowler when he put it on to drive downtown. He wove through traffic and people like a hungry shark in bloody waters. He left his car in a back alley where a cringing, fearful man came to meet him. The snitch told him something that made him smile before he plugged him. From there he made a trip over to a big warehouse with dirty windows. He stood outside and watched a bunch of bootleggers pouring cut hooch into cheap bottles before slipping away.

Relief flooded through Nellie. Dapper believed he had finally located the operation of a rival bootlegger called Two-Time Matteo. Cutting his bathtub swill twice allegedly gave Two-Time his moniker, but his cheaper prices had been rumored to be putting the squeeze on Jackie. Nobody did that and kept breathing. The hit would go down tonight, and Facelli, who liked to watch Dapper make an example of a rival, would be there.

Time to make like the canary.

Nellie cradled her drink between the long loops of her pearls as she considered her options. She'd never called the Cap from inside the club, but this couldn't wait. There were only two phones in the joint: one in Jackie's office and one in the kitchen.

Slowly she turned around, setting her sights on the rawboned kid mopping up behind the bar. He was new, nervous, and probably had never talked to a girl. When he caught her watching him, he flinched, making the sweat beads dotting his forehead trickle down into his eyes. He used his knuckles to smear away salty tears before he looked back and smiled too wide.

Nellie had him. Then all it took was a tip of her glass, a little scream and a dash around to collide with the kid.

"Oh, oh," she said, clutching his narrow shoulders and pressing herself against him.

From his worn shirt she got an image of

him leaving a tenement house and stepping over a pile of garbage, and quickly shut the door in her head.

Poor, stupid, and desperate to make some dough.

"You okay, Miss?" he asked, his voice a twanging string.

"I spilled hooch all over my dress, can you believe it?" She took a dollar from her clutch and tucked it in his hand. "There's a sink back there, maybe I can sponge it down?"

The kid stuttered and stammered something like *yeah, sure,* and *this way* before leading her back into the kitchen.

Just as Nellie had hoped the dinner cooks had already gone for the night, leaving her alone with the kid, whose eyes were still skittering up and down her.

"You're a real life saver, fella." She decided against kissing his cheek. If she did, he'd never leave. She sauntered over to the sink. "Give a girl a minute to fix herself up?" She tossed him a smoldering glance over her shoulder. "Then maybe you can buy me a drink."

Dazzled, the kid nodded, tripping as he hurried out. As soon as the swinging door closed Nellie dashed to the phone by the storeroom and dialed the operator.

"Police, First Precinct, right now," she demanded as soon as the girl answered, and then waited for the connection. When the desk sergeant's sleepy voice came on the line, she used her best lace-curtain Irish accent. "This is Bridget McMurphy. I got an emergency here. Put Cap on."

Every second of silence that passed on the other end had Nellie eyeing the door. At last a deep voice said, "What's the matter, darling?"

"It's our little man, sweetheart." She had to use code and the fake name so that everyone at the station thought she was Captain John McMurphy's wife. That kept her alive, and the cops that Jackie had on his payroll in the dark. "He kicked the dog and got fresh with me. He said he's gonna run off tonight with that friend of his, Mattie."

"All right." Cap sounded as relieved as she felt. "You just make yourself some tea now, Bridget. I'll be home in ten minutes to deal with our boy."

Nellie hung up the phone at once and rested her brow against the wall. Making tea was their code for the wrap-up of the sting. In less than an hour it would all be finished.

Jackie Facelli didn't know that Two-Time Matteo existed only in his imagination. The Bureau had worked hard to get the word out about him as the head of a bootlegging operation undercutting Facelli's business. Using Nellie's reports to shut down dozens of speakeasies, they'd first put the squeeze on those owners. Eager to avoid lengthy prison sentences, the owners had been coached into boasting to Facelli's men about buying cheaper hooch from Two-Time.

Finally, it had worked. Tonight, when Dapper and Facelli raided Two-Time's base of operations, they'd be walking into a Bureau trap.

Nellie knew how it would go down. Cap would get the BoP boys to the bogus bootleg site to wait for the killers and arrest them all. The murder of the snitch she'd read from the bowler would help Cap put pressure on Dapper until he pinned Mickie's murder on his boss to keep from swinging himself. Her brother's killer would spend the rest of his life in prison, and his boss would go to the rope.

She could stop now, leave New York City, and never look back. But where could she go?

Maybe back to the farm. The cows won't care what I did.

A cold hand clamped on her neck. "Never told me you were an Irishman's missus, Baby."

Nellie's heart clenched as she turned around, her pout in place. "Yeah, so I got a ball-and-chain, and a kid. Ain't my fault my ma can't wrangle the little man. Had to call his dad to come home from the factory." She stroked her fingers over his lapel, keeping the door in her head locked tight. "Bet you got a whole toolbox of little drillers by now, huh, Dapper?"

"Six." The hatchet man looked her over before he smiled, showing his tobacco-yellow teeth. "And one on the way."

He was buying her song and dance, and Nellie could almost breathe again. She'd make it out of here, alive and done with swimming in this cesspool. Then he grabbed her by the hair, and jerked her arm up behind her back.

"You're a snitch. Not even a good one." He marched her out of the kitchen and down along the bar toward Jackie's office.

"Don't be loony," she protested, hoping the fear in her voice sounded like a spoiled whine. "You know me, Dapper. I'm just looking to have a good time. Ask anybody."

He chuckled. "You know what Jackie does with sharpers? He gives them to me, so I can put the screws to them a while. Make sure we know everything you told the flatties. I got a warehouse out in Jersey that's nice and private." He halted and bent down, his stinking breath blasting her ear. "Gonna make you last a good, long while, Baby."

In that moment, Mickie's face floating behind her eyes, she couldn't pretend anymore.

"I *am* a copper, you boob," Nellie told him, jerking away from his mouth. "Bureau of Prohibition. You're under arrest for the murder of Michael Patrick Quinn. Now let me–"

A woman's shrill scream made Dapper swing around and go still. "Son of a bitch."

Nellie looked toward the screamer, and saw a dozen masked men rush through the narrow bookcase entry. *Droppers.* As the hired killers spread out and hefted their Tommy guns, Nellie knew she wasn't going to Jersey, or the farm, or anywhere ever again. Neither was anyone else in the speakeasy.

Staring at her death made her think of the one good thing about it: she'd sipped her last glass of watered-down hooch. She hated the stuff.

I'm sorry, Mickie.

Me, too, Sis, her brother whispered back.

The thugs began firing a spread across the club, their bullets smashing into screaming women and shouting men. Bodies fell like toppled trees along with the gore-spattered tables. Spilled booze formed little pools and rivers. Two musicians jumped from the stage to dance as gunfire hit them and riddled their bodies. Light bulbs smashed into showers of sparks, adding a festive air to the bloodbath.

Nellie saw Jackie run out of his office, his bodyguards on either side of him. They tried to make it to the back door, but all three men were cut down in a heartbeat. A bitter satisfaction flooded through her, as cold and heavy as dark water.

Got him, little brother.

As the guns swung toward her Nellie

instinctively tried to drop down behind the bar. With his bony hands Dapper held her tightly upright and in front of him. Only a moment before being pelted did she realize that he was using her like a shield.

Coward, hiding behind a skirt.

She kicked back, driving the heel of her shoe into his shin. His howl got lost as the droppers started firing at them.

Being drilled didn't hurt as much as Nellie had expected. Hot stings peppered her front, pummeling her like tiny fists. One that grazed her cheek made her head bounce back against Dapper's Adam's apple, making him choke. The pain came next, but even that seemed muted and far away. Knowing these men would leave here wrapped in body blankets left her feeling an odd emptiness, as if everything that had fed her hatred for so long had drained away.

Not so bad. Nellie didn't want to look down, so she looked at the broken bottles on the bar. The shattered glass reflected the exploding lights like little shooting stars. *Pretty. I should make a wish.*

When the killers charged across the club,

Dapper flung her to the floor. She heard him scream and fall a few feet from her, whining and gasping as he tried to crawl away. The acrid stink of gunpowder and spilled blood grew thick.

Bye, Dapper. Hope you suffer a good, long while before you bleed out.

All Nellie could do now was peer up at the tin ceiling and wait for the finish. For the first time she noticed that the punch patterns formed angels and stars. Was that heaven up there? More strange notions filled her head, probably from the blood loss, but she didn't mind. She wondered if she'd see Mickie or her folks once she left this world. She knew for sure she wouldn't be going where they had. She'd done too many awful, rotten things to get to Facelli, but that had been the price for her revenge.

It was done, and she was done. There was nothing left.

She could feel heat and wet pumping out of her many wounds, staining her pretty new dress. It made her hands and feet go cold, but Nellie wasn't scared. She felt sure that Hell was here, in this hard, cold world. The bootleggers and their mobs were the real devils. After she scrammed, it would probably be just like they always said: a big sleep.

Or maybe it'll be a place in Jersey, where Dapper will keep me forever.

A sad laugh stuttered out of her as Nellie realized the joke was on her. All she'd done had been for nothing. Some rival who hated Jackie had chilled off the louse for her. She could have stayed home and had her revenge anyway.

Mickie didn't say anything inside her head. He didn't have to.

She'd never let herself regret what she'd done for her brother and her folks, but the irony of this night gave her one last chance to mourn the life she hadn't lived.

I'd have spent my days soaking up the sunshine and looking after the herd. Every morning in the dairy, every night on the back porch watching the fireflies. Maybe I would have found a fella who cared enough to stick around and give me his ring.

The smell of copper made her open her eyes to see an enormous, brutally handsome thug crouching over her. He had wings, but he wasn't an angel, not with all those shivs strapped to his coppery feathers. Maybe he wasn't real at all, but then he picked her up, his claws cutting into her flesh. He sniffed her before he started touching her all over.

Nellie couldn't read people like things, and for once she was glad of it.

"Beat it…chump," she said, and coughed as something thick welled into her mouth. "Let a girl…kick off…in peace."

"Ah, but you've been a very bad girl, haven't you?" He brought her fingers to his pretty face, and then he licked the blood from them. "And a touch-reader. Born with your talent, too. That makes you worth taking."

She couldn't get enough breath to spit in his face. "I'm…already dead… stupid mug. Can't take…anything…from me."

"I'm taking you," he said, raising his fist.

As the demon punched his claws into her chest, Nellie knew then that she'd been wrong about Hell. So very wrong.

Chapter Twenty-Five

❦

COMING OUT OF the dream and seeing the thatched roof instead of punched tin made Nellie turn her head. Beside her Edane slept, his arm draped over her waist. The terror making her rigid fled, leaving her limp and relieved. She'd gotten out of the speakeasy of her dream. She'd come back to Scotland, to Dun Chaill, to the man she loved. She never had to go back to New York City, or the Bureau, or the farm.

Edane could be her home now.

As she reached for him the pearl necklace slithered over her wrist, caressing her, reminding her with its cool beauty of who she had been. Not that it was a bad thing. Edane knew fun, wild, carefree Nellie. He didn't know anything about the undercover bureau agent underneath the flapper.

How would he look at her when she took off Nellie once and for all?

Gently she nudged his arm until he stirred and rolled onto his side, freeing her. Rising and finding her clothes in the dark without waking him took some time. Once she had dressed, she tiptoed to the door. Looking back at Edane, she opened it and stepped outside. Whatever magic he had used to ward the greenhouse, it didn't wake him when someone left.

The borders of the night sky had taken on a dark blue tinge, telling her sunrise would come in another hour or so. She knew because she remembered sitting on the roof of her apartment building to watch the dawn arrive, imagining herself on the hill behind the milking barns. The boxy buildings of midtown Manhattan became the big walnut grove where she'd climbed trees with her little brother. The cars trundling along the cramped streets turned into the dairy herd, ambling along as they grazed in the wide pastures.

The rest of her memories of the country seemed vague and distant, as if she'd only dreamed about them a long time ago, or she'd tried not to remember them.

Whoever that girl was, you aren't her anymore.

Nellie did know one thing: she should have died in The Doll's Drum. Somehow that night the big demon had kept her alive and then healed her. The bullet wounds hadn't left a mark on her. It was as if they'd never happened. What she'd been through between being drilled in the speakeasy and falling into the glen still remained in the dark. But she sensed it had been a much longer stretch than her time pretending to be a good-time girl.

She reached for Edane's pearls as she recalled how she had talked and acted in the vision with the big demon.

Or maybe I kept playing the flapper, even after they took me. How long have I been living as Nellie?

At the barn she stopped to look up at the stronghold. She didn't hate or fear Dun Chaill anymore. That had come from the terror she'd brought with her from her time. She could see it was just a rundown castle with some interesting secrets. With her power she might help the clan locate and destroy all the old traps, and make it a safer place to live. Maybe she'd even find out what had happened to the demon that had built it.

A dark shape came out from behind the barn. "Edane gave you pearls."

Kiaran sounded almost polite, which made her smile a little. She'd been expecting him to come after her, but this time she wouldn't make a fuss.

"I didn't steal them, if that's what you mean." She watched one of his kestrels drop down to perch on his shoulder. "Were you watching the greenhouse?"

"Aye." He stroked the bird's head with gentle fingertips. "I ken you're no' in league with the demons, Mistress."

Now that did surprise her. "How do you figure that?'

"Broden told me how you refused him, and then made your heart naked to him. A spy wouldnae do thus." The kestrel released a sharp cry and flew off his shoulder. He frowned at the bird before he folded his arms and leaned back against the front barn wall. "Aye, and there's how you came to me in the passage, and bid me flee, when I'd chased you down with sword in hand. We might have burned together, there in the flames."

"You're welcome." His nice act didn't fool her any more than it had the bird. He wanted something. "So how come you're still tailing me?"

"You bedded him." Before she could reply he added, "I can smell him on you."

He didn't sound disgusted, exactly. More like disapproving. Like Mickie.

"It's okay. I'm going to make him marry me tomorrow." That didn't sound as funny as it had before, and she sighed. "I'm kidding. We're just having fun. You know, what people do when they're not being you."

"You ken naught about my brother." Kiaran pushed himself away from the wall. "Edane wasnae born with the strength or talent for the bow, nor would his sire teach him. He taught himself until he gained both. By will alone he took his place among us, and learned how to hunt. Since we attained immortality, he's devoted himself entirely to the clan. Alone he faced down a demon and a collapse to save you, but 'tis his nature. No man I ken possesses more courage or resolve."

Nellie caught a little hint of jealousy in his tone, too. "I may not know his life story, but I get that he's a great guy. Anyone can see that."

"Then look to yourself, Mistress," the falconer said. "You're lovely, but beneath the pretty skin you've no courage or honor. You use deception as easily as you laugh. You think of naught but yourself and your wonts. You yet use my brother as your slave. You claim you're having fun, but 'tis all you may offer him. 'Tis no room in your heart for Edane or this clan. You dinnae belong here."

Nothing tempted her to correct him, so Nellie remained silent until he walked away. She watched him enter the back of the stronghold, and then turned to retrace her steps to the greenhouse. She didn't hurry, for Kiaran's harsh words kept echoing in her head.

No courage or honor.

Kiaran would never like her. That much was clear. Even if she'd told him the truth about why she'd become the fun-loving flapper, it wouldn't absolve her in his eyes. On the contrary. He'd say it was proof of her nature.

And instead of being herself when she'd escaped the underworld, somehow, she'd come here as Nellie Quinn. The farm girl was gone. So was the bureau agent. Maybe she couldn't be anyone else now.

Maybe he's right about me.

Nellie knew the score. If she stayed at Dun Chaill Edane would be hers, but no matter what she did the clan would only tolerate her. Kiaran would definitely make sure of that. Domnall might keep the peace for a time—the chieftain had that knack—but eventually the other men would have to choose sides. That would divide them, and the contention would make Jenna and Rosealise resent her. The strain would grow until it became impossible for Nellie to stay, but her lover wouldn't let her leave without him.

Edane had been with these men for over a thousand years. She'd been a sparkle in his eye for less than a week. She couldn't take him from his family.

Instead of the greenhouse Nellie went to the stables, where she brought out and saddled the mare she'd planned to steal. For a moment she stroked the long rope of pearls with shaking fingers before she took it off and hung it beside the horse's empty stall.

Much as Nellie wanted to, she wouldn't steal Edane's dream. Maybe one day he'd find a gal worthy of him and his clan as well as his pearls. She hoped so.

Leading the mount outside, she pulled herself up into the saddle, and considered which direction to take. She felt eyes on her, and tugged on the reins to turn the mare away from the forest and toward the river. As she walked the horse past the kitchens, she saw a tall silhouette standing at the window.

This time Kiaran didn't chase after her.

Chapter Twenty-Six

✦

GALAN ROSE BEFORE dawn to search the skies, but clear weather again prevailed. He'd have to continue his search for the wench on horseback, crossing the highlands one plodding league at a time. Finding a mortal wench adept at trickery and theft would be the lesser of two difficult tasks. If the prince's half-brother still lived, he had remained so well-hidden that he'd never once been sensed by the other demons, just as they had never discovered where the Mag Raith now secreted themselves.

Could the hunters have somehow found the same means as the outcast had used to shroud their presence in the mortal realm?

In the barn Galan cast a ward over Fiana's bones to protect them in his absence, and then went to the stables to retrieve his mount. When he led the horse outside, he saw only a few demons standing sentinel, and two unfamiliar pack horses tethered to a post.

On the other side of the village a crowd of Sluath had gathered around one of the animal pens. Inside the fence Danar stood with two mortals in traveling robes.

Druids.

Tying his mount by the other two, Galan pulled his cloak hood up over his head and walked to the pen. Danar held each druid by the shoulder, and grinned as he listened to the suggestions being shouted by the other demons.

"Give them blades and have them fight."

"Toss them into the well. See if they float or sink."

"Make them use their magic on each other."

Galan shouldered his way to the fence to get a closer look at the pair. Both wore the unmarked robes of acolytes, and the similarity of their features and coloring suggested they were bloodkin. The taller of the two, however, had the calm, ancient eyes that came from many incarnations. This close he could also feel a hint of the power the older druid possessed, and something more: the sickly-sweet odor of flesh rot.

A willing sacrifice.

That druid had likely known this journey would end him.

"Tell me why you came here, and I'll let you live," Danar told the druids as he drew two of the long blades from his wings. "Or say nothing, and I'll cut off bits of you and feed them to my men."

The shorter acolyte's throat moved as he stared at the daggers, and then met the gaze of his companion.

"'Tis naught to fear, my son," the older druid said. "We shall meet again in the well of stars." He regarded the big demon. "We ken you dinnae dine on mortal flesh, *deamhan*. If you wish to end us, simply do so." He smiled. "Or we may do the work for you."

The acolyte took in a quick breath and turned, flinging himself against Danar. The *deamhanan* shouted and clouted him away, but not before the druid had impaled himself on one of his blades. His face emptied as he dropped to his knees and fell forward, driving the dagger to punch through the back of his robe.

Galan drew in the scent of the lad's blood and death, but unlike that of mortals it gave him no satisfaction. As quickly as the heat filled his head, it disappeared. When he opened his eyes, he saw the remaining druid scanning the faces of the demons as if looking for someone.

"Tell me why you came here," the big demon said, "or I'll blind you, cut out your tongue, and feed it to the swine."

"'Tis no need to torture me for that. You violated a sacred site near this village under our protection." The druid calmly folded his hands inside his robe's sleeves. "Our council sent me to speak with the one responsible."

The Sluath laughed and jeered at him before the big demon lifted his hand for silence.

"You think to punish the Sluath for trespassing, little tree-worshipper?" Danar leaned down to peer into his eyes. "It would not be wise to attempt a spell. Even now your life slips from your flesh."

"'Tis the way of the dying. We ken we might. My son didnae wish me to travel to the stars alone." At Galan's contemptuous sound the other druid turned his head to stare at him. "There you are. I bring a message for you from Bhaltair Flen, head of the druid council."

"My old friend has indeed risen high." Amused now, he pulled back his hood. "Deliver his message, then."

"For your evil acts against mortal and druid kind, you shall die a mortal death, and no' be permitted to reincarnate," the druid told him. "Surrender to Master Flen, and for the haven you once provided for his tribe, he shall assure you're given a quick and merciful end."

How like Bhaltair to repay a debt with vengeance. Galan flung off his cloak and leapt over the fence, summoning his power as he strode toward the druid.

"Aye, opening Fiana's grave, 'twas my doing. She belonged to me, no' Flen." He seized the druid by the throat. "Your cowardly master cannae threaten me. I'm beyond his reach now, but no' he from mine. Soon I shall hunt him down and tear the soul from his chest. Do you hear me?"

"Aye, as do the Gods," the druid choked out. "Surrender or you shall be damned for eternity, Aedth—"

The druid's neck snapped, and he went limp.

Galan stared into the ancient eyes, which sparkled for a moment as if with joy before they clouded and went flat. Dropping the body, he raised his boot and stomped on the young, slack face until it became unrecognizable.

The demons who had gathered around the fence grumbled bitterly as they wandered off to resume their posts. Danar bent to turn over the younger druid and yanked his dagger from his belly.

Galan wiped the gore from his boot on the druid's robe before he regarded the big demon. "Now you shouldnae again doubt my loyalty."

"Find Nellie Quinn and you may take my place at the prince's side." Danar looked toward the south, breathing in deeply before he grinned broadly. "Don't ride out yet, Aedth. By sunset you'll not need the nag."

Although the skies remained clear, a subtle change in the air made the wings on Galan's back itch to spread. Then he knew what the big demon sensed. "A storm comes."

Chapter Twenty-Seven

WAKING UP TO find himself alone in the greenhouse had Edane on his feet in a heartbeat. He tugged on his trousers and boots and tossed his tunic over his shoulder before he hurried out. The ward he'd cast remained undisturbed. No one had taken her in the night. She'd left.

A tired-looking Broden intercepted him on the way to the stronghold. "She's gone, Brother."

Edane shook his head. "From my arms, aye, but Nellie wouldnae–" The sight of the pearl necklace in Broden's fist silenced him. "Where found you that?"

"The stables," the trapper told him.

"Hung by the stall of the mare she took. She went through the forest to the river, and crossed it. I reckon the lass rides for Wachvale."

The jolt of shock soon faded as Edane thought quickly. He had seen the strangeness in her eyes last night, and had felt her shake just before she'd gone to sleep. Now what he'd assumed to be weariness took on a darker meaning. Something had frightened her, and from her pure delight in loving him it had not been that.

Nellie remembered something more. Something that made her run from me.

"Tell the chieftain I go to find her," Edane told Broden.

The trapper looked as if he might say more, and then nodded and handed him the pearls before heading into the stronghold.

Edane ran to his chamber to collect his best bow and his sword. Stuffing his largest quiver with iron-tipped arrows, he strapped it to his hip. He had lost his taste for the hunt long ago, but in him burned a new desire. If the demons came for his lady, he would strew the glen with their pretty carcasses.

As he made to leave through the kitchens, he found Rosealise waiting with a packed satchel.

"Our stores have not been touched, so I believe Mistress Quinn left without food or water." The housekeeper then offered him a small cloak. "I made this to fit her. It's still rather cool after dark."

"My thanks, Lady Rosealise." Nellie's lack of provisions now plagued him. If she found her way through the ridges past Wachvale, she could travel any of a dozen trails or roads into the midlands, but she'd find little water and no food.

Domnall and Mael met him at the stables, and as he saddled his horse the chieftain said, "We'll summon the others and ride with you, Brother."

"After last night, you cannae leave your mates or the stronghold unprotected." He swung up onto his mount. "'Tis best I go alone. Mayhap if Nellie sees 'tis only me, she'll no' hide or run. We've much to settle between us."

The seneschal tied his mate's satchel to a saddle loop. "Signal with a fire if you find you need the clan. We'll bring our ladies with us."

Edane clapped the big man on the shoulder before he rode out of the stables and galloped toward the river. Once he'd crossed the rushing currents, he picked up the mare's tracks, which angled to the north side of the glen before following the edge of the forest.

He urged his horse into a hard run toward Wachvale. The spell boundary surrounded the abandoned village, but ended just beyond it. Edane knew once past the protective barrier the demons might find Nellie, as the scout had when she'd fallen into the pasturelands. What would convince her to take such a risk?

At last he approached the long stone wall dividing the glen from the now-empty pasturelands, and saw the thorny wooden gate to the village standing open. Beyond it the missing mare placidly grazed on the high sweet clover. Seeing the hobble and saddle left on her reassured and dismayed him all at once. Nellie had made sure the mare would not wander away, yet she hadn't finished riding.

Edane walked his horse through the gate, dismounted and closed it. The thorns from the bramble branches covering the gates pricked his palms, but the shredded empty ties atop them gave him pause. When they'd come to gather the livestock left behind to starve, he hadn't bothered to go into the village itself. He had seen the pink and white crystal spiral ward left behind on the gate.

Someone had since removed it.

Weather and time had scattered much of the remains of the once-prosperous village, leaving only a few charred stone hearths squatting on blackened earth. He left his mount hobbled beside the mare, and walked between two mounds of scorched slats. The sense of walking over burial ground came over him as he passed odd pits scoured shallow and smooth by the wind.

Between them he saw the small boot prints that Nellie had left. Her trail went from the pits across the three-sided village green, and into the only structure left standing: a tall, narrow drying shed with walls made of stone. He walked past the village well and approached it, slowing his step only when he thought of her power.

Everything Nellie touched told her its past.

Coming here meant seeing the horrors inflicted by the plague. Edane stopped just outside the shed.

"My lady, 'tis me. I ken you must be... Will you come out?" When no reply came, he peered inside at the shadowy interior. "I wish only to see that you're well."

"Sure, have a look." Nellie's voice sounded tired and dull as she emerged. Soot begrimed her boots and streaked down the front of her garments. In her hand she held a piece of dirty wool. "I should have kept riding, but I thought..." Her brows drew together as she glanced around her. "Food. I stopped because I needed food."

"You read what the plague did to the villagers." He wanted to hold her in his arms, but something in her manner held him back. "'Twas a terrible thing."

"None of them got sick." She met his gaze, anger burning the confusion from her eyes. "That druid who bossed you around—Galan—he brought a bunch of thugs here. They murdered most of these people, and set fire to the houses. Then the demons came and culled the thugs. I saw everything they did."

Sickened by the revelation, Edane reached out and touched the wool she still held. "Then Galan shall be made to answer for it."

"When they left a few people were still alive." She knotted her fist around the cloth. "Something else came and killed them, and then dragged away all the bodies. It looked like it was made of shadows."

❦

THE FEEL of death clung to Nellie even after Edane had taken her to the communal well so she could wash. Maybe it was the coldness of the water as he poured it over her hands, or the soot from all the burned things she had touched still on her clothes. Reliving the slaughter from the villager's homes and possessions had been worse than anything she'd picked up from the walls of Dun Chaill. She definitely couldn't live here, not after seeing that shadow monster, but she couldn't return to the castle either.

Are we having fun yet? the cold voice sneered inside her head.

"The creature made of shadows, 'twas

likely Galan," Edane told her. "To enter the village unseen, he may have cloaked himself with a darkness ward. Ending the few living and hiding the bodies would also conceal what he did here."

"Yeah, well, I'm not staying here." Nellie watched him dry her hands with the edge of his tartan. "And I'm not going back with you. I don't belong at the castle. I need to find my own place." Far, far away from you, she added silently.

"'Tis an old shepherd's hut on the south side of the pastures, near where the stream bends, inside the spell boundary. 'Twould serve as a place for you to shelter and sleep for a time." He nodded toward the glen. "I'll take you there, if you wish."

Edane was stalling so he could find out why she'd left, Nellie guessed, but that was fine with her. She wouldn't put the finger on Kiaran. From the beginning the falconer had seen through her like she was made of glass. He'd always been honest with her, too, which was more than she could say. How could she blame Kiaran for wanting to protect his people? Maybe if she'd done a better job of that, she would have never gotten into this mess.

As they walked from the village to where the horses waited, Nellie saw the bulging satchel tied to Edane's saddle. "You packed for a long trip."

He shook his head. "Lady Rosealise sent provisions for you, and this."

The housekeeper probably didn't want her back either, Nellie thought, until Edane took out a small cloak and draped it over her shoulders. Of finely woven, light brown wool, it had intricate gold and green embroidered birds around the collar. Nellie recognized the fabric and threads. The housekeeper had been saving them to make herself a winter gown.

Thanks, Rosealise, she thought as she stroked a finger over the stitching, and saw the housekeeper secretly working on the cloak by candlelight. She'd miss the Englishwoman and her generous heart. And Jenna. And the guys.

Not Kiaran.

Once in the saddle Nellie rode with Edane along the wall until the end. From there he guided her through a birch grove to where the river narrowed to a curving stream. Sunlight sparkled on the rushing currents, reminding her of the new dress she'd worn on the night she'd gotten shot. Flowers covered the banks so densely they looked carpeted in blue, violet and white velvet.

"'Tis a safe spot," Edane told her, and pointed across the stream. "The boundary ends where the firs stand."

Tucked up against some old oaks on this side of the water she saw a squat thatched hut with mossy walls. A barrel stood beneath one corner of the roof, still brimming with rain water. A small circle of stones surrounded a tall swatch of grass under a trio of twigs, which she guessed was an overgrown campfire. The shelter looked very primitive, but the roof appeared intact, and a door of bark layered between willow branches still guarded the entry.

Edane helped her down before leading the horses to the stream to drink. That gave Nellie a chance to look inside the shelter, and to stop thinking about how it felt to have his hands on her. Hides covered the two small windows, but had been scraped thin to allow in some light. A fleece-stuffed mattress atop some woven branches occupied one corner, and a chair-high stump sat next to two others with a large flat stone propped atop them.

The interior smelled faintly of sheep, but the dirt floor had been packed down, and she didn't see any signs of mice or bugs. With a little work she could make it livable. From what she remembered of her walk-up in the city, it had been pretty close to this.

The shepherd must have washed in the stream and cooked over a fire, so she could do the same, at least until she emptied the satchel. After that she'd have to find food. Maybe she could fish or gather berries. She also had no idea of how to do those things, but she could teach herself. She wasn't helpless.

Or maybe I'll starve.

Nellie walked out of the hut to find Edane crouched down, snapping twigs and tossing them into the circle of stones. Somehow, he thought he could make her change her mind by not trying to change her mind. He was indulging her, like she was a child having a tantrum.

"You don't have to do that," she told him. "I can take care of myself."

"You've a fire steel?" he asked as he worked his dagger against the end of one stick to curl thin layers of wood. When she shook her head, he tossed a small pouch to her. "Keep mine."

Nellie gripped the pouch and made her voice cold as she said, "I don't need you here. Go back to your clan."

"As you wish." He dropped the curled stick on top of the twigs and stood. "Farewell, my lady."

Edane started walking toward the tethered horses as if he meant to do just that. He was going to ride back to Dun Chaill, and leave her here alone, and she wasn't going to stop him. She just had to make sure he wouldn't return.

"I'm not a lady," she shouted after him, furious now. "I'm not a flapper. My name isn't Nellie. Everything you think you know about me is a lie."

Chapter Twenty-Eight

DISCOVERING THE MAG Raith had renewed their search of the stronghold had made Cul reinforce the wards protecting his underground lair. Wherever they chose to look, they would find nothing hidden or buried but stone, dirt, or the debris of centuries. Should they test the illusions, they would behave as if real. The scent bundles he had scattered around the keepe would also provide the correct smells for their noses.

To his relief, the only intruder who could expose his subterfuge had conveniently left in the night.

Although he hated leaving the castle unattended, Nellie Quinn's abrupt departure provided too great a lure for Cul to resist. Although his injuries from the collapse had yet to completely heal, he left just before dawn. He tracked her to the empty village, and for a time watched her use her power to discover its secrets. The cloaking ward he had used when he'd killed the remaining mortals and disposed of all the bodies had been a thoughtful precaution. She would never know it had been him. Still, her power exposed another secret that needed keeping.

If I don't silence her, the entire clan will come to search for the bodies.

While his work at Dun Chaill remained safely hidden, they would surely find what he had long concealed in the caves above the village.

Feeling Nellie's despair as she wandered through Wachvale surprised Cul, for he had been sure the demons had leeched her dry. It made him hungry for more, but as he crept down toward the village he saw a red-haired warrior approaching on horseback. He looked determined and hopeful, a man in love pursuing his lady.

Edane mag Raith had come to rescue the damned wench yet again.

His unwanted arrival drove Cul back into the shadows of the ridges. Nellie would have been simple to kill, but an immortal shaman would not fall victim so easily. If he could manage to snuff the life out of them, he'd have to drag their bodies off to the deep shaft he had used for the villagers. The same would have to be done for their horses, or the Mag Raith would move their search to Wachvale and look to the ridges.

Cul knew that in his weakened state Edane just might prevail over him.

A rumble of distant thunder interrupted his musings, and Cul looked out to the darkening horizon. It had been nearly sevenday since a storm had threatened the highlands, and he knew when it reached the Sluath they would not be able to resist it. He looked down again as the archer led Nellie from the village and helped her onto her horse. Instead of riding back toward Dun Chaill, he took her across the pastureland toward the stream.

Cul fumed. They would remain here for a time, doubtless to coo at each other. Then he recalled that an old shepherd's hut lay just inside the boundary, and an answer to his dilemma began to form. It would provide them with shelter from the storm, if he could somehow keep them there until it arrived.

Did he dare an attack on two fronts?

He climbed higher, moving north through the craggy ridges until he came to the shimmering wall of his spell boundary. Caressing the curtain of magic with his gnarled hand, he summoned his power and channeled it into the ancient barrier. Slowly he reached through it until his hands emerged on the other side.

The spell he cast belonged to Edane mag Raith and, like the storm, it raced out toward the Sluath-occupied village.

Closing the spell barrier, Cul cast over himself a shadow ward, and began his long climb down from the ridges.

Chapter Twenty-Nine

EDANE TURNED AROUND to face Nellie. The anguish in her eyes made him long to go to her and take her into his arms, but he forced himself to stand his ground. She needed more than comfort now. She needed his understanding, even if she didn't realize it yet.

Mayhap even forgiveness. We never offered her that.

"You've remembered your past, then?"

"Yeah, I did." She marched up to him and shoved the fire steel pouch into his hands. "My real name is Helen. Helen Frances Quinn."

The imposing sound made him smile a little. "'Tis splendid."

"Yeah, well, I wasn't. I was a bumpkin. I

grew up on a dairy farm in the country." Her mouth twisted. "That's how I know about cows. I spent most of my life around them. Be sure to tell Broden that. He was wondering."

Edane pocketed the pouch. "We've no' much knowledge of cattle. Yours could help the clan better care for our stock."

Nellie made an exasperated sound and stalked off toward the stream. He followed her, and thought of what more he might coax from her. She sat down with a thump in a bed of wild bluebells and pansies. Lowering himself down a handspan away from her, he stretched out his long legs and watched her as she stared at the flashing currents.

"I'd ken more of your life on this farm," he said.

"I lived with my parents and my younger brother, Michael. We called him Mickie for short." She cradled her knees with her arms. "He was a good kid, and such a clown. No matter what kind of mood I was in, he could always make me laugh. I adored him. Everyone did."

He saw the tears glinting on her lashes. "If 'tis too painful to speak of your brother–"

"That will never change." She took in a shaky breath. "As Mickie and I got older, we took on more work for our folks. We knew how to run the farm, and planned to do that together once they retired. But sometimes I wondered if we would. See, Mickie loved driving our delivery truck to the bottling factory. He'd come back and tell me about everything he saw in the city. It seemed so exciting to him, compared to life on the farm."

Sunlight streamed down on her, gilding her curls until it looked as if she wore a caplet of golden lace. It glided along her fine skin, painting the tiny fine hairs on her arms white. But for all her beauty it was her voice that reached into him, and wrapped around his heart.

Edane knew then that it didn't matter to him who Helen had been, or why she'd become Nellie. He loved this woman.

"One day my brother drove to the city to make a delivery, but he never came home. The next morning the constable came." She brushed away the tears from her eyes, and the emotion left her voice. "I heard my mother's screaming from the barn, and ran to the house with my father. They found Mickie, dead on the side of the road, next to a broken-down truck. He'd been shot. He was only seventeen years old."

Pain so filled her that she couldn't allow herself to feel it, Edane thought, a tactic he'd used himself in his mortal life. "I'm so sorry, my lady."

"When I went to the police station to collect my brother's belongings, I talked them into letting me see the broken-down truck." She looked down at her hands. "What I really wanted to do was touch it, so I could see who killed my brother. Mickey had stopped that night on the road to see if he could help. The men who had broken down were bootleggers. They killed him so they could steal his delivery truck and use it to move their hooch."

Edane was stunned. "You had your power before the Sluath captured you?"

She nodded. "I just saw flashes when I was a little girl, but as I grew up more came to me. It got so that I had to wear gloves whenever I left the farm. That day, when I used it to see Mickie's murder, I knew what I had to do. I applied to the Bureau of Prohibition to become an agent, a copper who hunts bootleggers, so I could find the men who killed my brother, and make them pay."

Her hands collected more blue bells and pansies as she told him of the final loss she'd suffered after leaving the farm. Both her mother and father had been devastated by their loss, far more deeply than Helen had realized. While she was away at the training academy they fell into melancholy and neglected themselves. It rendered them too weak to fight off the sickness that came that winter, when they had died within a day of each other.

"The last time I went home to the farm, I had to bury my parents next to Mickie." She looked down at the bouquet she'd made, and wound a piece of grass around the stalks. "The doctor said it was the flu, but when I touched things in the house, I felt their pain. They wanted to be with my brother more than they wanted to live. Everyone I loved was gone. I had nothing left but revenge, and I wasn't giving that up."

She told him how she returned to the academy to finish her training as an undercover agent. They taught her how to pose as a flapper so she could help locate underground clubs that served spirits against the law, and then sent her to live in the city as Nellie Quinn. Her ruse also allowed her to secretly use her power to identify and track the man she'd seen kill Mickie.

"It took a year of haunting the speakeasies, but I finally found Mickie's killer, and his bootlegger boss. We set up a trap for them." She stood up and carried the bouquet down to the edge of the water, her shoulders rigid now. "In the end, though, it was all for nothing."

Edane stood and went to her as she lifted the bouquet to her face. "Dinnae tell me they escaped."

"No. One of the boss's rivals sent droppers to kill everyone at the club. No one got out alive that night, except me." She tossed the flowers into the stream. "That big Sluath, Danar, found me dying. He knew about my power, and shoved his claws into my chest and that's all I remember." She pressed a hand over her heart.

He reached out and turned her to face

him. "Now tell me why you left Dun Chaill last night, for I cannae fathom your reason. You remember a past spent seeking justice for a terrible wrong done you, and that drove you from me?"

"That's the thing. It wasn't an act." She touched his cheek, her face pale now. "Don't you get it? I would have done anything to get even, and I did. I flirted and drank and danced with horrible men. Thugs and thieves and killers. I made them think I wanted them so I could touch the things they carried. I let them put their hands and mouths on me. I lied to them, stole from them, and even drugged a few when I had to get away fast. I had so much hatred in my heart, Edane, that I would have done worse."

Now he understood. "You're wrong."

"Ask Kiaran when you go back." She stepped away from him. "He'll tell you exactly who I am, and why you need to stay away from me. I think he's always known."

Edane thought of the vision they had shared, and knew he had to try to reach that part of her— the part she'd locked away in her time.

"Give me your hand, my lady," he said, and saw her brows draw together. "Only for a moment, and then I shall go."

Though she pressed her lips into a thin line, she slowly reached out to him.

He took her hand, pressed her palm to his skinwork, and curled his hand around her nape. Summoning his shamanic power, he sent magic into his arm and hand.

The sunlight grew blinding, and then everything faded to white.

IN THE DEPTHS of the underworld, Nellie heard the arrival of the demons from the outer tunnels. They didn't make much noise, but the cries and screams from their captives came through the walls. She got up and went to stand at the fang-shaped panel of glass that was her only window. Since moving her into the new digs, the Sluath had given her a front-row seat to their fun and games. Through it she could see the other poor chumps that had been dragged out of time as they arrived, like a herd under black skies.

Watching them come back always made her sick, but Nellie had no choice. Danar had said that if she didn't "attend our return from every cull" he'd nail her up against the window so she couldn't turn away. Seeing what they did was supposed to make her like it. That much she'd worked out on her own.

She'd have to compliment the big goon when he came to gloat.

Nice work, Boss. Must have been a real chore, grabbing a bunch of maroons who couldn't fight you off.

Judging by their expressions, the captives being herded in by the guards still thought it was some kind of mistake or nightmare or afterlife. Nellie had gone through that, too, although she'd quickly gotten wise to how this place worked. Everything she touched in the underworld gave her the inside scoop. She'd used that knowledge to try an escape through the tunnels, but she hadn't known that Danar could track her through the tattoo on her neck.

This time I will not punish you, the big demon had said as he dragged her back. *Run again and I will cut off your hands.*

Outside the window a demon yanked a fine lady in a poofy gown from the very back of the group. He began to beat her while she screamed and pleaded for help. The other Sluath froze the newcomers so they couldn't do anything but watch as her skull cracked open and blood poured down her silks.

Dead before she hit the ground, her body melted into the rock.

The mortals always assumed the demons would do the same to them if they stepped out of line, so everyone in the cull got quiet and cooperative. Nellie had seen the con a thousand times, and the cruelty of it still gnawed at her. Like so much in this place the fine lady wasn't real. She existed only to have her head split open and scare the new arrivals.

The Sluath would never waste a real dame that way. They liked to make them last.

The sound of the wall dissolving tempted Nellie to turn around, but it might have been another test. She'd been put through too many to make mistakes anymore. Then there came a wet thump and a very human-sounding groan. She smelled blood and man, which meant it was real. They could fake everything down here but stink, or maybe they wanted to con her into thinking that.

She'd learned the hard way never to underestimate her captors, especially now, when she had gotten close to finding a way out.

"I've brought you a gift, little reader," Danar said, his cold breath touching her branded neck and making the ink burn. "Don't you want to look at it?"

"You yammered about me watching the culled come through," she reminded him, doing her best to sound bored. "I stop, you spike me to the wall, see?"

"See this." He yanked her around by the arm.

A thin boy with long red hair sprawled by her bed. He dripped all over from the hosing he'd gotten, and his chest heaved as if he were having trouble breathing. From his trousers she guessed he was from one of the olden times. He'd been tattooed with Danar's mark along the arm, which meant he belonged to the big Sluath now. Not good, considering the shape he was in. Danar liked his slaves feisty. They earned him more in the arena and the pit.

If she was going to help the boy, she had to act like Nellie, who wouldn't have given a damn.

"You're giving me a mostly dead guy?" Nellie looked up into the demon's coppery eyes and feigned a yawn. "Jeepers, I didn't get you anything. Let me go catch a cockroach."

Danar flashed his fangs as he laughed. "This one was too far gone for the arena when he came, but I mended him enough to serve. He's yours to do with as you please until the next cull."

In all the years she'd been here he'd never given her a slave of her own. Not a good sign.

"What a pal." She made a show of sauntering over to the boy, who on closer inspection turned out to be a slender young man. He looked up at her, his vivid blue eyes filled with despair, and she glared at him before she turned to pout at Danar. "Say, what's the price tag? You fellas gonna watch me do him?" She'd rather stab herself with one of his wing blades.

"We'd rather feed." He waved his claws

over the glass, which disappeared into the wall. "Indulge yourself well with this one, Nellie, and I may reward you again."

She gave him a lascivious smile. "Sure thing, boss."

Danar was expecting her to make whoopee with the guy, also not comforting. Sex slaves were only given to mortals in the final stages of transition. She was pretty sure that was supposed to push them over the edge to make their first cull.

As soon as the big demon left through the wall Nellie dropped down and helped the man to his feet.

"Upsy-daisy." She had to half-drag him onto the bed, but once he was on it, she covered him up and brushed the sopping hair back from his lean face. "I'm not going to hurt you, okay? No matter what the big lug said. Just keep your voice low. If we make too much noise, they'll come in so they can watch me hurt you. Got it?"

"Be ye a demoness?" the dazed man croaked in a heavy accent.

At least he speaks English.

"Nope," she assured him, and then saw

how he was shivering. "I'm going to get into bed with you, but just to warm you up. Don't hit me."

It had been so long since she'd touched another human being that sliding under the blanket and gathering him close made her heart pound with nerves. His body felt almost ice-cold, likely from whatever Danar had done to fix him. If he hadn't been so weak, she would have sworn he was in transition. As her feeble body heat warmed him his stiff limbs relaxed, although he still looked at her as if she might bite off his face.

She didn't blame him. Being here for so long had made her look a lot more gorgeous than she'd ever been in her time. The last time Danar had allowed her to look in a mirror, she'd been so beautiful she'd screamed.

"My real name is Helen," she murmured to him. "I was gunned down in my time before the demons grabbed me and brought me here."

He blinked a few times. "Ye cannae be evil, surely."

That was a question she couldn't answer without a whole lot of story that he'd never understand, so she shrugged. "I'm working on it. What's your name?"

"Edane mag Raith." He took hold of her hand. "Helen, 'tis no' a Pritani name."

"I'm from New York, in the U.S. of A." His name sounded as pretty as he looked, and she was definitely feeling warmer now, too. *Do not make whoopee with the mostly-dead guy,* Nellie told herself sternly. "What's a Pritani?"

"The name of my people." He lifted his head and took in the swanky prison chamber they'd given her this time, but he didn't seem interested in the banquet table or the huge sunken bath. "Four hunters came with me. They're as my brothers. Where went they?"

"If they were brought here, they're slaves now, like you." She didn't know how else to tell him that hard truth. "Every mortal who comes here is enslaved."

Edane's mouth tightened. "But no' ye?"

"I was, at first. They've been using me to read things… Ah, that's a long story. They also want me to change into a demon, like them, but I'm not who they think. I'm still like you." She hoped. Every day it got harder to hang onto that. "Where did they take you?"

"On the hunt," he said and grimaced. "'Twas my doing." He reached out with one of his shaking hands, and touched the curl on her cheek. "How long since ye were enslaved, Helen?"

"Call me Nellie." She didn't want to explain that. "I've been here about a hundred years. Time moves slower in this place. I think they can keep us alive almost forever if they want, but most slaves don't last too long. A lot of them go crazy."

"We must find my brothers and with them escape this place," Edane said, and sat up. "'Tis no' where they belong."

"Keep it down." She checked the wall portal. "We can't bust out of here without help, but there's someone I think might. It's dicey, though. This bird is a strange one."

He frowned. "Bird?"

Nellie put her lips next to his ear to whisper, "There's a demon who wants out of here, too."

Chapter Thirty

※

THE SLUATH PRISON chamber faded, and Nellie found herself staring at Edane as he took his hand away from her. They stood together in the flowers by the stream, just as they had before the vision. Pleasure and pain twined inside her as she looked up at the sky, which had darkened with storm clouds coming in from the west. The last rays of the sunset dusted them and the trees with orange and gold.

How could she feel like this, as if the world were falling apart around her, in this beautiful place with him?

Edane stepped close to her, his eyes intent

on her face. "You saw me brought to you in the vision?"

Nellie could only nod. Now she wished she'd never remembered anything. It had been so much worse than she could have imagined. She'd spent a hundred years as a Sluath captive. What had they done to her all that time? Why was she still alive?

They kept me from aging, just like they kept me from dying.

"Now you ken. 'Twas Helen who held me in her arms to warm me when I came to the underworld," Edane told her. "Helen who promised to help me and my brothers escape. Being Nellie, 'twas a ruse for the demons, just as 'twas for the men who killed your brother."

What he said had to be true, but Helen seemed like someone else to her.

"I was Nellie when I came here. At least, being her was all I remembered. I don't think I'm Helen anymore." But even as she said it, she realized Nellie's anger and conniving had gone. "Who am I supposed to be now?"

"You must choose that, my lady." He bent to her, whispering a kiss so soft on her lips she barely felt it. "Come now. We should build a fire and make a meal. There shall be no chance when the storm comes."

Nellie went with him, numb from the revelations of the vision. Edane showed her how to use the fire steel, and then took out oatcakes and smoked fish from the satchel. He shared the food and a waterskin with her as the stars came out, and then draped her with her new cloak.

The way he looked after her made her wonder about their time together in the underworld. They'd become lovers, that much seemed sure, but had they fallen for each other? Was it happening again because their hearts remembered it, even if their heads didn't? Was that why she'd wanted him so badly, and still did?

And who did Edane really want, Helen or Nellie? He only knew Nellie.

"You neednae choose now," he said, startling her as he offered her one of Rosealise's scones. "You remember why you continued your ruse. The rest shall come in time."

"Hope so." She broke the little biscuit in

half and handed one piece back to him. "How did you know we would share another vision?"

"I didnae," he admitted. "I recalled how we touched the first time we summoned our memories. I reckoned I'd try the same again with my magic." He frowned. "'Tis odd. More time passed in this vision than at the castle."

The touching, her hand on his arm and his hand on her neck, made sense. "If we do that again, could we see more of what happened to us?"

"No," Edane declared, sounding almost angry as he got to his feet. "'Tis enough that you saved me and my brothers. You've seen into your heart. You're a good, kind lass."

"I was a good copper. I'm the cat's meow at lying. Kind, ah, I need to work at that a bit." She looked up at him, and saw guilt on his face. "You don't want to remember any more, do you? Why not? You've already seen me at my Nellie worst."

He took his bow and checked the string before shouldering it. "'Tis naught to do with you, my lady."

Yeah, she figured that much. "All right, I'll

guess. I'm good at that, too. In the vision you said that it was your fault the demons took you and the others. Was it because you were hurt? Because they always go for people like that. I was pumped full of lead when they snatched me."

He tossed another piece of wood on the fire, and stared at the sparks flying up for so long she thought he wouldn't answer.

Finally, Edane faced her. "I defied the Gods and refused to become a shaman. My magic, 'twas their gift to me, so that I might follow the path of faith and healing. I wanted none of that. If I couldnae be an archer, I didnae wish to live. For that they damned all five of us."

"Whoa, hey, now." Nellie stood and took his hands in hers. "I don't know about your Gods or your beliefs, but what you did doesn't sound so bad. Why would they punish all of you because you chose not to be a shaman?"

"I went on a last hunt with my brothers." Edane smiled sadly. "One from which I didnae intend to return."

As Edane walked with Nellie to show her the stars, he found himself describing how sickly he'd been as a lad. It had been centuries since his mortal life, and as he told her he still felt the frustration of being unable to run or play without growing dizzy and losing his breath.

"'Tis why I'm different from the other Mag Raith," he admitted. "As a mortal my affliction left me too thin and frail for warrior training. I never grew as the other lads."

"I like you the way you are," she told him, slipping her hand in his. "I mean, the other guys seem nice enough, but they're too big. A girl my size has to worry about getting squashed, you know?"

"Aye." He rarely felt the envy he'd once suffered by comparing himself to the other hunters, but she'd given him a new reason to feel content with his lack of bulk. "That you neednae worry with me."

"So what does any of that have to do with you being damned?"

"'Twas decided I should be trained by the tribe's shaman. He taught me healing, and awakened the magic inside me, but I despised my power. I wished to be an archer." He stopped in a meadow of wildflowers by a large flat rock, and sat down there with her. "I went into the forest to practice the bow, and teach myself what my sire wouldnae permit. There I met Domnall and the others, and joined their hunts in secret."

"Sneaky." She bumped her shoulder against his. "Must have made you a good hunter."

"'Twas no' as difficult for me, hunting on horseback. The mount ran for me. The shaman gave me herbs that made my breathing easier, and kept my head clear." He pressed her hand between his. "I used them to keep my weakness from my brothers, and hid my hunting from the shaman. Yet my affliction grew worse."

"Guess you couldn't hide it forever, huh?" Nellie said softly.

"I reckoned I could, but no." Edane traced the ovals of her fingernails. "One night I returned from a hunt with game for the shaman. I wished no more training, and I'd decided to show him proof of the archer I'd become, so he would release me. Outside his *broch* my heart began to beat strangely, and then seemed to clench like a fist. Then came pain, so deep in my chest I couldnae take in a single breath. I felt my life fading. I dropped to the ground, and all went black."

He told her of how the shaman had found and dragged him inside, and forced a bitter potion made with witch's thimble down his throat. It had brought him back from the edge of death, and eased the terrible pain in his chest. Then came the truth that had been kept from him since his boyhood.

'Tis yer heart, lad. The old man's hand had felt cold against Edane's flesh, which he had painted with protective spirals. *'Tis damaged and 'twill ever falter when ye burden yerself. 'Tis why ye wouldnae thrive as a bairn, nor grow as other lads. Now 'twill do thus again unless ye give up yer bow. Ye cannae hunt again.*

Edane had blinked back an unmanly surge of tears. *I'm no' a shaman.*

'Tis no' yer say, the old man said flatly. *The bow cannae serve ye now, lad. Use yer Gods-given power. They give ye this night as a warning. Go ye again with the hunters, and ye shall die.*

"What he said that night came as no great surprise," he admitted. "Even before my training with him, I'd long suspected 'twas that made me weak. I saw that I wasnae strong enough to hunt, and 'twas causing my heart to die. 'Twas naught else for me but to abandon the bow and my brothers. Yet I couldnae bear that. When I felt well again, I went and gathered more witch's thimble."

"Did you think it would keep you going?"

He shook his head. "A little may save a life, but too much stops the heart forever. 'Twas the latter I made into a death potion. I'd drink it after one last hunt, and die among my brothers as I had always wished to live: an archer."

"Oh, Edane." She embraced him, her cheek rubbing softly against his before she drew back. "You didn't take it, though, right? You wouldn't be here if you had."

"'Twas no' by choice." He looked up at the stars, which seemed so close he might touch them. "I never had the chance. When we took shelter at Dun Chaill from the storm, I lost my breath, and felt again that the end had come. The rest, 'tis yet lost to me."

He glanced up to see the edge of the storm just over them. He'd lived under the shadow of death for so long as a mortal that his life had been much the same: a feeble light about to be snuffed out.

"This rock is cold," Nellie said and took off her cloak. She spread it on the grass before she sat down on it, and held out her hand. "Come here."

Edane saw she wished to comfort him, but he shook his head. "I ken what I did, my lady. 'Tis my greatest shame. You cannae understand."

"I'm a farm girl who became a copper and a lying, thieving floozy to find the mugs who killed my brother. Who knows what I did with the Sluath? Then I conned you and the clan, the only people who helped me. Shame and I are old, old pals." She patted the cloak. "Park it right here, come on."

Reluctantly he joined her. She pushed him down on his back, and then stretched out beside him.

"Do you believe your Gods are up there?" Nellie asked after they had watched the stars for a time.

"I dinnae ken. The shaman claimed they're all around us, in every part of the world." He glanced at her. "Why?"

"Just wondering." She turned and lay her arm across his chest. "Was the shaman the one who said they'd punish you for becoming an archer?"

"He claimed that the Gods didnae bestow a gift to see it squandered," Edane admitted. "And when he learned I'd taken up the bow, he warned that I'd be forever damned for my defiance."

"Huh." Nellie put her hand over his heart. "Like I said, I don't know anything about your Gods, but it sounds like the old guy did all the talking."

Edane nodded. "He often spoke for the Gods."

"Sure, that's the job, right?" She drew a line with her finger from his heart to his mouth. "He already knew you had a bad ticker. He wanted to train you so you could take over for him. What would scare you into giving up hunting? I'm thinking the Gods."

He frowned. "'Tis no a jesting matter, my lady."

"Sorry. I'm just a little confused. So which thing were you damned for? Going on that hunt or planning to kill yourself?" she persisted.

He'd never considered that. "I cannae say."

"It's strange. I mean, you went on lots of hunts before that last one, but you didn't get damned until that night. Why would the Gods wait?" She tapped her finger against her lips. "Of course, you brought the heart-stopping potion along, but you didn't take it, so they couldn't stick you for that."

Edane had to warn her that speaking of the Gods with such flippancy could bring down their wrath. Yet before he spoke, he realized that such a belief, like all the others he held, had been ingrained in him by the old shaman.

"Here's how it shakes out for me: you did defy the old guy for a while, but in the end, he got what he wanted," Nellie said as she propped herself on his chest. "You don't hunt anymore, you're not going to die, and you're the clan's shaman. Pretty good con if you ask me."

A chuckle escaped him, which grew into laughter. Nellie caught it with her lips, kissing him through the mirth until the first raindrops came down to pelt them. Edane sat up with her, intent on taking her back to the shelter, but her hands gripped his shoulders.

"No, let's stay." She wrapped her hands around his neck. "I love the rain. I love this place." She leaned in to kiss him again, and against his mouth she whispered, "And I love you."

Thunder rumbled over their heads, and Edane felt his heart swell. "Say that again."

"I love you. That's who I am. The woman who loves you." Her head dropped back and she closed her eyes, her voice rising to a shout. "I love this guy."

Edane held her as the storm unleashed a heavy downpour that soaked them in seconds. Nellie laughed and shook her wet curls and tackled him against her now-sopping cloak. The power of the storm merged with the passion rising in him, and Edane held her close as he began to change and more memories flooded into him.

"You told me to go without you." He

reached for her nape, stopping just before touching it. "In the underworld."

Nellie gripped his arm. "Show me."

Chapter Thirty-One

***

THE APPROACHING STORM caused great agitation among most of the Sluath, for whom being earth-bound seemed the worst of torments. Galan found it amusing that the guards and sentries spent more time watching the slow-moving cloud bank than the village and the ridges. Danar clouted several as he derided them for ignoring their duty, but even he seemed slightly distracted.

Galan's own excitement swelled as the storm swallowed the sinking sun, and billowed into mountains of tumorous darkness. There seemed to be no end to the tempest, and if it raged on for days he could spend all of them on wing.

Prince Iolar remained alone with his two attendants for much of the day, emerging from his cottage to order Seabhag to remove their bodies. He took in the darkening skies before eyeing the other demons, who watched him with the stillness of the starved at a feast.

"Secure the mortals that still serve us," the prince told Danar. "You may remain behind with Clamhan to keep watch on them and our sanctuary."

The demon kept his skull mask in place, probably to hide his scowl, but the big demon merely inclined his head. "As you command, my prince."

With a casual wave of his hands Iolar removed his blood-spattered glamor, revealing his majestic white and gold beauty. As he did Galan felt the brush of his power, which stirred his own. Ever since the prince had revealed the limits of his abilities, Galan's fear of him had not reawakened. He even admired the clever ways he used terror to control his unruly army.

Iolar might be the most powerful Sluath, but he had weaknesses as well. His vicious temper, unrelenting vanity, and constant need for amusement could be used as weapons against him, once Galan acquired more power.

"I believe I'll go find more females for my personal use. I can carry at least two or three at a time, more if they're not fully grown." Iolar yawned before catching Galan's gaze. "When I'm finished collecting, I expect to see Nellie Quinn among your captives, Aedth."

"Then mayhap Danar should hunt with me, my prince," Galan told him. "For I've never seen the wench."

The prince's golden eyes shifted as he studied his face. "Danar is needed here. I will hunt with you, Druid."

Before Galan could reply Iolar sauntered off to inspect the pen where the two druids had died.

"Our prince bestows a great honor on you, Aedth," Danar said, seizing his arm and marching him toward the barn. "Come and I shall arm you myself."

Galan didn't resist until they were out of the prince's sight. "I dinnae need your blades, *deamhan*."

"The prince suspects something, or he

would not leave me behind and hunt with you." Danar shoved him inside the barn. "If he learns that the halfling may yet live, he will go mad with fury. We'll all be made to hunt for him, day and night, from the sky and the ground. He'll not stop until every Sluath drops or he kills them. I cannot permit that."

"I hadnae planned to reveal your lies." Galan smiled smugly. "But now you make me think of your place, serving our prince. 'Tis a position of great trust and of considerable value. Since you so fear Iolar's wrath, I reckon it should be mine."

Danar loomed over him. "Do not think to threaten me when you remain mortal enough to kill. There won't be enough left of you to collect in a bag."

"How shall you explain that?" Galan countered. "I've done naught but as I'm ordered. I've sacrificed my tribe, my body, even my future lives for the prince. I killed one of my kind to protect both of you. While you? You've lied to him about the creature he most hates. Now you speak as if you mean to end him, and that I cannae allow." As the demon drew a huge dagger from the top of his wing,

Galan held up one hand. "After I'm gone, he shall ken what you've done. I've seen to it."

Slow clapping came from behind them, and Galan turned to see the prince leaning against the inside of the barn wall.

"Most impressive," Iolar said, not to him but to Danar. "I find myself utterly dazzled by your brilliance. Go and prepare the brethren for our hunt. I will deal with Aedth."

The big demon sheathed his blade, bowed to the prince and departed.

Galan summoned his power, although he knew it to be no match for Iolar's. "'Twas all trickery. You and Danar sought to deceive me with this tale of a halfling. Why?"

"Danar has been watching you since the attempt on my life," Iolar said, smiling. "It's his job to protect me and my throne, and he lost his trust in you, if he ever had any. He anticipated your demand to resurrect your wife, and advised me accordingly. Be assured it was not all lies, Aedth. I had a halfling brother who could bring the dead back to life. When I took power I killed him and had his stinking carcass dumped into a time stream. I have no idea where or when his body landed in the mortal realm, but he's long since rotted."

All the fury emptied from Galan as he saw what a fool he'd been. "You sought to drive me mad before you ended me."

"We had to know what you were." The prince advanced on him. "Danar felt convinced that you wanted me dead. Once in his confidence, he thought you would attempt to conspire with him to assassinate me. I believed you would turn on him and use his fear to take his position. I'm quite pleased you proved me right." He lifted his hands, his power forming two golden orbs around his claws. "Kneel, Galan."

His knees buckled, but not to please the prince. He had lost Fiana, and with her his own chance at immortality.

Snow and frost swirled through the barn as Iolar cast his power over him. The front of Galan's tunic tore open, and new glyphs were etched in black across his chest. The magic within them sank into his body, and spread through him, colder than the ice crusting his face. He could feel it hardening his bones and freezing his blood. It felt like death, and yet when the power faded he felt his chest rise and air rush into his lungs.

"I have given you power no mortal has ever possessed," the prince told him. "Use it to serve me well, and when we return to the underworld, I will make you an immortal. There we will breed more halflings until we create one with the power to revive the dead."

Galan rose unsteadily, unbalanced as much by his promise as the wings that shot out from his back. "You would do that?"

"To have again slaves who may never truly die?" Iolar's teeth glittered like polished bones. "To that end I will sire ten thousand brats myself. Come."

Galan could feel the power of the storm rising over the village. As never before it called to him, wordless and wild, pulling at the new power inside him. He followed Iolar outside, where Danar waited.

"The *deamhanan* stand ready, my prince," the big demon said.

"Make your apologies to Galan," Iolar said before he spread his wings and soared up into the sky. The other Sluath followed in a wide, glittering swath against the roiling dark gray clouds.

"Dinnae waste your breath," Galan told Danar as he started to speak. "All you've done shows how greatly you wish to be rid of me. I shallnae forget that, nor give you the means to try again."

"If I wanted you dead, Aedth, you would be rotting in the ground." His copper eyes flashed with amusement. "To serve as I do demands absolute allegiance to Prince Iolar, and none have ever challenged my place at his side. For him to bestow so much on one who remains mortal has troubled me."

"'Twas envy," Galan said, gloating now. "The prince favors me with wings, and his power, and now the promise of immortality. When we go to the underworld, I willnae take your place. I shall make my own."

Danar chuckled. "Perhaps you will. You've already done the impossible."

He would have told Danar to fack himself, but in that moment the seeking spell he had cast earlier returned to him with a captured burst of Pritani magic. He lifted his hands to contain it, and between his palms appeared the blackened remains of a ravaged village. Two figures on horseback appeared to be riding across the pasture beyond the ruins. One had long red hair, wore a green and black tartan, and carried a bow and quiver.

"Edane mag Raith cast a spell no' an hour past," Galan said. "From Wachvale."

Danar peered at the image before it faded. "That wench with him is Nellie Quinn."

Chapter Thirty-Two

THE GLEN BLURRED around Edane as the connection they shared wrenched them from the storm, and hurled them into a colder, darker place. Long tunnels filled with strange stone stretched out all around him. The rock moved with light and color, as if a living thing. It cast an unnatural glow over him and Nellie as they stood together, waiting. A hooded figure approached them, its robes flowing as it glided through the air.

"'Tis naught to discuss." Edane stepped between the demon and his lady, his hands bunching. "She goes with us."

Behind him the stone drew from his fears

and flashed images of a shrieking flapper being torn apart by vultures.

"Cut it out," Nellie said, slapping the rock face. The gruesome tableau vanished.

"Nellie cannot leave the underworld," the Sluath chided. "My brethren have held her captive for more than a century." A thin gloved hand gestured toward the dark stone. "As you see, she has been altered too much by her time among the Sluath."

"Then I shall stay with her," Edane said flatly. "Send my brothers and their ladies through, and leave us."

"Give us a minute, huh?" Nellie said to the Sluath. When the demon floated away, she put her arm across his shoulders. "Truth time. I'm not like the others, or you guys. All the time I've been here has changed me. There's almost nothing left of the girl I was."

"I ken you," Edane told her flatly. "You're good and kind. You've saved us all."

"The little good I've done since you came doesn't make up for what I did to get here." She touched his cheek. "I've earned this hand, Danny."

"Fack that." He pulled her into his arms,

pressing her against his chest. "I willnae go without you. You're my life." He looked over her damp curls to the demon, who had returned. "You claimed that love saved you, Sluath. 'Twill be the same for Nellie. She has my heart."

"That shall not stop her from reverting," the Sluath warned. "When she emerges from the time stream, she will awake as the woman she was when she was culled."

"You ken what Danar shall do to her when they find us gone. Leaving her here, 'tis certain death." Edane cradled his lover's face in his hands. "We shall find each other again, just as the others shall. When we do,' twill be as 'twas here."

"You're such a maroon," Nellie sighed, and pressed her cheek against his chest before she stepped back and gave a little nod.

Edane felt the demon's cold hand on his nape and stiffened before he plummeted into darkness.

༺༻

Nellie dragged Edane onto the sky bridge

while the demon set the lever. She could feel the faintest stroke of awareness on her neck, which meant that Danar was stirring. "Have all the others gone through now?"

"Yes. He's the last before I enter the stream." The demon sounded as bland as ever. "You've no regrets in loving this rebel?"

"Why, are you worried about your honey bunny?" She looked up as the Sluath hovered closer. "Oh, come on. When you really love someone, you'll give up everything for them. What you want, what you could be, even your life. I've done it twice now." She glanced down at the archer. "No regrets this time. You?"

The demon sighed. "If I could feel them… No, I think not."

"There you go. Okay, time to scram, Danny," she said, grunting the words as she lugged him over to the edge above the cloud stream. "You find yourself a sweet gal out there. She'll love you as much as I do, I'm sure, and don't take any wooden nickels, you goof."

Looking down at his face made tears rush into her eyes. The sensation felt strange. Nellie hadn't cried in decades.

She turned as the demon floated over to her. "Make him forget everything about me and this dump," she managed to say as the tears began to fall. She swiped angrily at them. "*Everything.*"

The demon touched its claws to Edane's brow, and dark blue magic flared for a moment. "Send him now."

With a sob Nellie pushed her love off the bridge, and watched the cloud stream drag him through the time portal. It felt as if something small and fragile inside her finally uttered one last gasp and died. Only when he'd disappeared from sight did she take out the dagger she'd stolen from Danar.

She'd always known this was her only way out.

With her free hand she felt along her side until she found the space between the two ribs nearest her heart. She'd stab herself, and her body would fall into the time stream. Maybe she'd land back in her own time, in the little cemetery next to Mickie and her folks. Not that it would matter to anyone but her.

"You could live forever if you remain here, and become Sluath," the demon said. "Even now, you stand just on the brink. I could take from you every memory of what you did to help the rebels, and me."

"Yeah, well, after being with him, I'd rather die." She heard the sound of distant groans and nodded toward the stream. "They're starting to wake up. You'd better hightail it out of here."

"Perhaps I'm wrong." Claws snatched the blade out of her grip. "Love may be enough to save you."

Before Nellie could blink the demon touched her forehead. A black cloud billowed inside her head, wiping out every memory, every thought, until all that remained was her name.

"Deserve *this* hand, Nellie Quinn," the demon murmured, and then shoved her off the bridge.

Chapter Thirty-Three

NELLIE FELL THROUGH time, through shadows and memories, through herself in all her lives. She saw the peaceful stillness of the farm, the shrouded emptiness of the speakeasy, and even the glaring white prison chamber she'd shared with Edane. Each place seemed to be waiting for her, as if she could go back to them if she wished.

Instead she opened her eyes, almost blinded by rain as she looked at Edane. She had conned him in the underworld, too, but it had been for the very best reasons.

"You'd have ended yourself," he said, as if he couldn't believe it. "But for the demon, and love."

"Just like you." She tried to smile. "Think we're both damned now?"

He hauled her against him, kissing her so deeply she bowed back over his arm. She clutched at him, dragging him down on top of her as the rain pounded over them. Their hands tangled as they tore at their clothes, her nails grazing his hard abdomen as she jerked down his trousers. He shoved her skirts to her waist and tore apart her knickers, spreading her thighs as he pushed between them.

Then he thrust into her, hard and pulsing with his need, and Nellie uttered a long, heartfelt moan.

"Never again shall you leave me," Edane said through clenched teeth. He worked in and out of her pussy with powerful, passionate strokes. "No more lies, or cons, or sacrifices. You'll return to the stronghold and mate with me and love me as I love you. Or I think I shall end us both."

"Sounds swell." Nellie gripped his hips, pulling him deeper inside her. "The loving and mating you, I mean. Let's quit trying to kill ourselves, okay?"

Rain poured down the sides of his face as

he stared down at her. "You'll be my wife? Truly?"

"Sure." She slipped her hand inside his trousers to caress the tight curves of his buttocks. "You gotta make an honest woman out of me." When he frowned, she added, "I never went this far when I was undercover. Before that, I never had a guy of my own. You're the first man I've ever loved, body and soul."

"The first." He seemed dazed now.

"First and last." Nellie tightened her muscles inside to gently squeeze his shaft. "You're the only man I'll ever love."

Edane covered her mouth with his, and as the storm raged on he pumped into her over and over. She came on the pounding strokes of his cock, her cries scattering her delight through the thunderous deluge. He didn't stop until he made her insane with pleasure a second time, and watched her shake herself apart with it before he stiffened and joined her.

Nellie groaned as she felt him flood her fluttering, clenching softness, the thick warmth spreading inside her like the love pouring from her heart. She'd have this, and him, for the rest of her life. They'd have to make peace with Kiaran, and tell the clan what had happened in the underworld, but she knew that nothing would ever come between them again.

By the time Edane shifted them onto their sides rain had plastered their hair and clothes to them, and the cloak beneath them was more puddle than wool. He held her close as he tried to straighten her skirt and his trousers.

"I don't think it's going to stop." She held a hand over her eyes to look up at the storm. "Want to head back to the shelter? We can try this again naked and dry."

He laughed and helped her to her feet before he turned away to retrieve the cloak. "Aye, my lady, but first we must–"

Something slammed into the back of his head, and he fell into the mud.

Sharp claws sank into Nellie's shoulders, snatching her off her feet into a shroud of shadows. As she screamed, the Sluath clamped his hand over her face, and soared up into the storm with her.

Chapter Thirty-Four

DOMNALL JOINED MAEL at his tower observation post. Rain poured all around them from the partially-finished roof, and the jagged arcs of lightning showed flashes of the worry on his face.

"He shall find her and bring her back to us," the chieftain said. "I'll stand the watch. Your lady awaits."

"Aye, as does your Jenna." The seneschal sounded distant as he peered out toward the glen. With his power he could stretch his senses across great distances. "'Tis something amiss, yet I've seen naught but the rain and the night."

Domnall had felt restless for most of the

day as well, but he'd blamed that on allowing the archer to pursue his lady alone. He knew Mael to be particularly sensitive to trouble, however, and trusted his instincts.

"Do we gather the clan and ride after the lad?"

The big man caught his breath. "Two arrows." He pointed in the direction of the abandoned village, where two faint streaks of flame arched through the storm. A third came after and between them, which clarified the signal's meaning. "Sluath."

No more had to be said. They left the tower at a run and called for Kiaran and Broden as they passed the great hall. In the kitchens Mael quickly told his wife of the archer's signal, and she hurried off to fetch Jenna.

Neither of the women had the power to fly like the Mag Raith, but Domnall had made double saddles for two of the mounts. As he assessed his hunters, he saw Broden offer the ladies long iron daggers. Jenna tucked one in her belt next to the short cudgel she had brought.

"I would make a pitiable duelist, my dear

sir," Rosealise told him, shaking her head and then producing a bundle from her skirt pocket. "These contain sand and thorns, however, which are quite unpleasant when flung in the eyes."

Once they mounted the horses Domnall led the clan out of the stables and out into the open ground in front of the stronghold. There the men and their mounts began to glow as the storm infused them with power. When they rode forth, the horses' hooves left the ground and they ascended into the wild night sky.

Domnall signaled the men to take positions behind Mael to conceal their number as they approached the glen. The seneschal used hand signals to indicate movement toward the north, and then wheeled around with his sword ready, as a fast-moving silhouette intercepted them from the opposite direction.

"Hold," Edane shouted as he reined in his mount to hover. "The demons clouted me and took Nellie into the ridges, there. They dropped out of sight near the old caves."

"How many?" Domnall asked.

"Ten. Galan and the prince among them."

The archer met his gaze, his own filled with fury. "If he harms her, I shall have that *druwid's* facking head."

"They must need her alive for something," Jenna said, "or they wouldn't have grabbed her."

"We shall see what we may." Kiaran held out his gauntlet, and the two kestrels perched on it took to wing and flew off toward the ridges.

Domnall signaled for the men to fly to the ground, but as soon they landed Edane made to ride up into the slopes. He reached out and grabbed his reins to stop him. "No, brother. You saw but ten. 'Tis likely more may await in hiding. We must be canny now. Let the raptors look for us."

The archer's eyes narrowed. "You wish me to trust in the bastart who drove my lady from Dun Chaill?" He glared at Kiaran. "You saw her go in the night, didnae you? And glad of that, said naught."

"'Tis no' the time, lad," Mael said gently. "Later we shall settle that. Now we must rout the demons, and save your lass."

A darkly-glowing figure with the face of a

skull plunged down from the sky, narrowly missing the seneschal's face with his claws before he flew up and away.

They had been spotted. Now they had no choice but to pursue the Sluath before the demon revealed their presence to his infernal brethren.

"After him," Domnall said.

Chapter Thirty-Five

NELLIE KNEW BETTER than to struggle as the cloaked demon dragged her into a cave and flung her at the feet of a man she'd seen in her visions. He was bigger than she'd realized, and now had wings on his back. He also radiated the kind of power she'd only known to come from the Sluath.

You've been a very evil boy, she thought, grimly trying to hold onto some hope. She knew the demon had hurt Edane, but he also healed quickly. The storm might revive him pretty quickly, too. Could he track her through the sky? *Probably not.*

If Nellie was going to survive, she needed to be smart and buy him some time.

"The elusive touch-reader." Galan Aedth jerked her to her feet and looked all over her, smiling as he took in her bedraggled dress. "You've accomplished much for such a small wench."

"Thanks, Pop." She smiled lazily at him. "Want to lend me a cloak? I'm freezing here."

"Give that bitch to me."

Nellie looked over at the demon who had snatched her, who now dropped his ward to reveal his white and gold beauty. Iolar gazed back at her without his usual smirk, and then snatched at her with his claws. Before he could grab her, the winged druid hauled her out of reach.

"I want her now, Aedth," the Sluath prince said, baring his teeth.

"As soon as she has read the stone, my prince, she shall be yours."

Though Iolar began to advance on them, a slim *deamhan* wearing a skull mask hurtled into the cave, coming between them. Nellie recognized Clamhan, who barely managed to stop before colliding with the prince.

"The Mag Raith," the demon said, his wings still extended and fluttering. "They–"

"Where?" the prince demanded. He shoved him toward the entrance. "Show me." He paused and eyed Galan. "Wait for my signal."

As she watched them go, Nellie's heart almost beat out of her chest. Edane was here. But in the next instant, Galan bent her arm behind her back, and used the painful hold to march her into one of the tunnels.

Nellie didn't want to be alone with the druid, but she'd take him over the prince any day. "You can make me touch anything you want. I don't have to say a word about what I see."

"Truth." He stopped in front of a solid wall of rough stone that sparkled with magic. "Yet I'll wager you dinnae need your eyes to use your gift." He drew a blade and waved the tip in front of her face. "Which shall I cut out first? Or mayhap this." He shifted the edge of the blade to press against her nostrils. "Shall the archer wish to fack you again with the nose sliced from your face?"

"Okay, okay." Nellie held up her hands as if surrendering. "Show me what to read."

He shoved her toward the wall, and as

soon as she got within a few inches the magic warding it reached out to her with dark power. It had been bespelled to kill a mortal, just like the other gates to the underworld, but this one had also been sealed.

"Sorry, boss," she told the druid. "If I touch this, I'll be dead before I can say a word, and you get nothing. Then I think the prince kills you for wasting me."

Galan shoved her down on her knees. "'Tis why you'll read the floor of the cave."

Nellie uttered a forlorn sigh, but as he brandished the blade again, she stretched out her hands over the rock beneath her. When she detected no sense of magic extending from the gate, she touched the rough surface.

Dun Chaill's monster appeared in front of her, a torch in his fist shedding firelight over his scarred, distorted body. In his other hand he held a strange little rock that he moved back and forth over the open portal, which filled in with stone as he muttered in a language that sounded exactly like the one Edane used when he cast his spells.

He looked different now, almost human, at least until he turned to face her.

Her jaw dropped as she saw his pale white skin beneath the grime and scars, and the peculiar color and slant of his yellow eyes. His crippled limbs had human muscles under the demonic skin. His face looked eerily like Iolar's, if someone had beaten the prince with a tire iron.

"Well?" Galan demanded.

Nellie described the demon to him, skipping only the fact that she had seen him at the Mag Raiths' castle.

"He's kind of wrecked, and can't walk really fast. You could probably catch him easy."

She hoped he'd try, anyway. The monster would snap him in two and pick his jagged teeth with the pieces.

"Culvar lives," the druid muttered. He glanced back at the tunnel before he jerked her to her feet. "What of the spell he cast?"

"He waved around a pebble the size of my thumb that oozed gunk which changed colors." That was the only way to describe it. "He also said some stuff, but not in English. It started with—"

"Silence," Galan hissed and pressed the tip

of his blade against her lips. "Repeat naught of what you saw here or I shall cut out your tongue before I slit your throat."

Horse feathers, Nellie thought as she tried to look frightened. She could see the feverish greed in his eyes. *You're not going to let anything happen to me.*

Chapter Thirty-Six

FEAR AND FURY warred inside Edane, who guided his mount with his knees as he held his bow ready. He and the clan used what cover the trails leading up into the ridges provided before the slopes grew too steep for the horses. They either had to fly or go on foot, and with the demons' advantage of the higher ground both presented myriad perils. The sky provided ample room to fight, but no cover. They could use the ground and the storm to disguise their approach, but if more than ten demons awaited them they had no means of hasty escape.

Kiaran halted beside him, and pointed to a dark recess between two outcroppings.

"They hold Mistress Quinn in that cave there. Four guard the opening from the front, two from above, the rest scattered in the brush."

Domnall eased Jenna to the ground with one strong arm and glanced over at Mael, who did the same with his lady. "You ken what to do."

She gripped his hand tightly, nodding before she and Rosealise disappeared into the brush.

The chieftain studied the terrain around the cave before regarding Edane and his men. "'Twill be as a boar hunt. Kiaran shall draw out the swine between our blinds there." He pointed at two wide swaths of brush directly below the cave. "Mael and I shall attack from cover. Broden, you and the kestrels shall come in from the sky to strike from above. Edane, use the fight as cover to go in and retrieve the lass. Dinnae linger to seek vengeance. As soon as we've freed her, we go."

"Galan shall be waiting with her," the falconer warned. "And another. Dive saw her taken inside by a cloaked demon."

Edane nodded, tamping down the urge to

plow his fist into Kiaran's unconcerned features.

Before he took to the sky, Broden touched Edane's shoulder, and nodded to the chieftain. A moment later he flew up and took cover behind a stand of thick evergreens, where the kestrels followed and perched in the branches. The other hunters rode up into the brush, where Kiaran dismounted and crept toward the cave.

Edane guided his mount into position behind the falconer. The chieftain's scheme seemed sound, but his unease grew. They had yet encountered no patrols or sentinels. The druid may have brought only a handful of demons that had scattered too far to spot their approach, but that seemed unlikely. Galan had been proud and conniving, but never foolish.

The wrinkled face of the old shaman appeared behind Edane's eyes.

The bow cannae serve ye now, lad. Use yer Gods-given power.

In battle? Though his fist tightened on the bow, Edane forced himself to close his eyes and drew on his magic to stretch his senses.

He could hear the clan now, moving

almost soundlessly into position. The ink on his arm burned as at last he sensed Nellie, her presence muted by the druid but growing stronger. She was coming out of the cave with him, but Kiaran had strayed too close to conceal himself.

Edane leapt down from his mount, holding his bow ready. He rushed through the brush to reach the cave before the druid spotted the falconer. But as he did, he spied a demon preparing to hurl a spear at Domnall.

'Tis a trap.

His bow string made a soft sound as Edane released his first arrow. A heartbeat later it pierced the Sluath's throat, silencing him. His second arrow thudded into his chest, and the third into his brow. The demon collapsed behind the chieftain, who seized the spear and made a sharp sound as he threw it at Mael.

The seneschal ducked, and the spear impaled a demon reaching for his neck.

Kestrels screamed as a bolt of power flung Kiaran back, and the Sluath prince descended in front of the cave.

"Take them," he shouted, and more demons erupted from the brush.

Edane's hands flew as he pulled the iron-tipped arrows from his quiver and shot every demon he saw closing in on the Mag Raith. A demon hurled himself at his bow, but Broden snatched him from the air and flung him to the ground.

No sooner had he hit the dirt than Rosealise darted forward from behind a large tree. She threw something from a small bundle into the demon's face, causing him to cry out. He turned and stumbled, groping for her, just as Jenna emerged from the tree trunk. She plunged an iron dagger into his back.

From the ground Kiaran groaned as Edane stepped in front of him, notching three arrows on his bow as he aimed directly at the prince's head.

"You ken what I did to your scout," he told the Sluath. "Give me the lass."

Broden flew down towing two horses, and flung the reins to Mael and Domnall. The three took to the skies and began fighting the demons who had survived Edane's arrows. Ash and blood began to color the rain.

"I remember you: the weakling. Danar advised against tormenting you. You barely survived the portal." The prince smiled, his beauty glowing like a thousand white suns. "I watched you with her in the glen. Does she still make you call her Mistress when you fuck her? As I recall you became quite taken with the scheming little bitch."

"Give her to me, and live," Edane said, feeling strangely calm. "Keep talking, and die."

"No." Kiaran managed to haul himself to his feet and join him, his sword unsteady in his hand. "He's mine."

"Ah, now the half-dead one and the weakling would vie for the right to fight me. Am I to be flattered or depressed?" Iolar snapped his fingers, and Galan emerged from the cave with Nellie, who looked pale but otherwise unharmed. "I suggest a trade, Shaman. The slut for my treasure."

"I've no treasure but her." All around him Edane heard his clan battling the demons, but he didn't take his eyes off the prince. "Release my lady."

"Oh, dear," Iolar sighed. "Really, I do you a favor now." He snapped his fingers again. "Cut her throat, Galan."

The druid suddenly doubled over, and Nellie broke away from him. The prince snatched at her as she ran past him, and his claws ripped through her dress, but she twisted free. As she raced toward him Edane swung his bow sideways and released his arrows in a spread that would strike both Iolar and Galan.

The druid straightened and flung a bolt of power at the arrows. They curved in the air, reversing direction before they flew back at Edane and Kiaran, their iron tips glowing with lethal magic.

Too late Edane saw through the cunning ruse. The druid had never been injured. He and the prince had wanted him to let loose his arrows. But when Nellie glanced over her shoulder, the unexpected took them all by surprise.

"No," Edane yelled.

Nellie flung herself in front of them like a shield. Her small body jolted as all three arrows struck her from behind.

Kiaran cursed as Edane dropped his bow and caught her in his arms. He looked up to see Galan and Iolar take flight, soaring up between the demons and the Mag Raith until the clouds swallowed them. A few moments later the Sluath that were still able to fly followed their prince.

Falling to his knees, Edane held Nellie against his heart. She looked up at him, her eyes filling not with pain but relief—and love. He looked up at the falconer, desperate now.

"We must take her back to Dun Chaill. 'Twill save her, as it did our ladies."

"Iron…arrows," Nellie gasped. Her face grew ashen as she took a shallow breath. Wisps of smoke drifted up from her back. "Not much human anymore. Won't work."

"No, you're still mortal," Edane told her. "You must fight again, my *peyrl*. Fight for me, for us. Stay with me."

"Tell Jen, the watcher," she whispered. "His name…Culvar. He's…"

The breath escaped from her, but did not return.

Edane flipped her over, and jerked his arrows from her flesh, which was blackening and smoldering. That meant nothing to him. The demons could not have her. Death could not have her. She was his.

"She didn't change completely," he told Kiaran. "I can still save her. Get me a horse."

Kiaran looked up and suddenly shoved him aside, knocking him to the ground. As Edane scrambled up, ready to kill him, the pale body of a naked woman fell atop Nellie's and went limp.

As the rest of the clan converged on them, Broden jumped down from his horse, seizing the woman who had fallen. She had such pale blonde hair it resembled moonlight, and skin so white it looked snowy. Sluath glyphs ran from the front of her shoulder and over her left breast to her waist. The trapper gently lifted her from Nellie, and Edane saw blood all over her back. Domnall pressed a finger to the side of her neck.

"She yet lives," he told Broden.

Domnall looked down at Nellie's still face, and then met Edane's gaze. "We ride for Dun Chaill."

Chapter Thirty-Seven

BEING FORCED TO retreat from the Mag Raith, who had killed all but a handful of the demons escorting the prince, left all the Sluath in a vile mood. Galan watched Danar send the uninjured out to hunt as soon as they returned to the village. The wounded went to regenerate in the caves. The prince slaughtered two who would not survive the night, and then flew off to hunt by himself. The ever-devoted Danar followed him from a discreet distance.

Galan left the demons to their dismal grousing and tormenting of the handful of mortals still healthy enough to provide sport. In the barn he stripped out of his sopping garments and washed before donning his druid robes. As he did, he felt the strength of the new power suffusing him, still ready and eager to be put to use.

This night had been a disappointment for all but him. He now knew what would bring him his every desire.

He retrieved the satchel in which he had placed Fiana's bones, and carried them as he walked out into the night. Thanks to the lingering storm clouds he did not go to the stables, but stretched his wings and took to the air.

Flying his beloved from the village to a remote spot in the highlands gave him time to consider what he would do, now that he knew who had trapped the Sluath in the mortal realm. He understood the reason the creature had done so, for the same desire burned in him. Armed with that fire and his new knowledge, he would destroy the Mag Raith, and anyone who defied him.

It seemed a boon that Danar and Iolar no longer considered him a threat. That, too, would work in his favor.

In a spot too high for mortals to climb, and too desolate for anything to grow, Galan entered a remote cave where he had once collected crystals. The interior glittered with faint purple reflections. Gently he placed Fiana's bones in the center. Though he was tempted to linger over her, his new purpose would not wait. He exited and cast his power over the entrance, sealing it with rockfall.

"Sleep, my love," Galan said, resting his hand against the still-shifting rocks. "I shall return for you soon, and we will be reunited."

Now he would begin his search in earnest with but one goal: Culvar, the prince's halfling brother. The only Sluath with the power of resurrection, he would also undoubtedly possess a hatred of Iolar that Galan would be happy to indulge.

We had to know what you were, the prince had said to him.

If only the mighty Iolar knew how greatly he had changed.

Chapter Thirty-Eight

JENNA AND ROSEALISE hurried into the stronghold ahead of Edane and Broden, and brought blankets and bandages for the wounded woman. Carrying Nellie to a chair by the hearth, Edane sat down and held her. He knew he should be helping the clan tend to the pale lady, but he had to entreat the Gods for his own.

It had been so long since he had done so that he abandoned the usual honorifics. He spoke from his heart as he watched his lover's still, pallid features.

"I ken she's hardly mortal anymore. I saw the smoke rising from her wounds. But she died to save two lives. No demoness would do such."

Domnall came to stand beside him, and rested a hand on Nellie's head. He gave Edane a long look of silent understanding but slowly shook his head. The chieftain had seen the smoke as well. Edane's jaw tightened as he held Nellie closer.

Domnall moved to where the others were gathered around the wounded woman. "'Tis your lady there, Brother?"

Edane glanced over at Broden, who knelt beside the pale arrival, his expression that of a man in torment. His dark eyes flashed up for a moment, and he nodded.

"So much blood," Rosealise said as she gently sponged it from the lady's back, and then frowned. "I cannot find a wound on her. Jenna, will you help me turn her?"

The chieftain's wife reached out, but a white hand suddenly gripped her wrist and shoved her into the housekeeper. The pale-haired woman shot to her feet and grabbed Broden from behind. She pulled the dagger from his belt and held the blade to the scar across his throat.

"Non," the woman said. *"Reste en arriére."*

"Oh, crap," Jenna said as she helped Rosealise to her feet. "She doesn't speak English."

Edane looked to Domnall, who made a hand signal to Mael. Broden didn't move a muscle, but his eyes shifted from side to side.

"Mademoiselle," the housekeeper said, her tone soothing. *"N'aie pas peur. Nous sommes tes amis. Vous parlez anglais?"*

"Oui." The woman's gaze darted around, cool and assessing, but she didn't take the knife from Broden's throat. "England?"

"Scotland," Rosealise said. "Please, don't be alarmed. As I've said, we will not hurt you. We are your friends." When the woman pressed the blade deeper, causing blood to trickle along it, she added, "I did not say that correctly. We are strangers to you, but we mean you no harm. We found you and brought you here to help you."

"Stop moving, big man, I see you," the woman said to Mael without looking at him. "I see you all."

"Are you wounded, Mistress?" Domnall

asked her. "When we found you, 'twas blood on your back."

"No. My back is fine. I have a headache." Her gaze shifted to Nellie. "That one, she's dead?"

"No," Edane declared.

"Okay. *C'est bon.* Is good."

The woman slowly lowered the blade, and pushed Broden away from her. Her legs shook as she grabbed his tartan and wrapped it around her, keeping the dagger ready.

"What's your name?" Jenna asked tentatively.

"Mariena Douet." She swayed before she groped behind her. Finally she found the chieftain's chair and sat down heavily.

Rosealise approached her, stopping when she lifted the dagger. "Let us help you, my dear lady. You've been through a terrible time."

"No. If you touch me again, any of you, I will kill you." The blade then fell from her hand to the floor, and she slumped to one side, unconscious.

Broden slowly bent down to retrieve the bloody dagger, and then backed away from the Frenchwoman. "She's forgotten." His mouth shaped the last word, *me*, as he touched the cut on his throat.

"Like our other ladies," Domnall said, "in time Mistress Douet shall remember." He exchanged a look with his seneschal. "I want something understood by all of you. Those who escape the Sluath shall be made welcome by this clan. Even if they hold a blade to our throats."

Jenna blew out a breath. "For now, let's hide all the weapons so we can get some clothes on mademoiselle and put her to bed."

As the other clan members busied themselves, Broden hesitated as he passed Edane. With a gentle touch that the archer would never have expected, the trapper briefly placed a hand on his shoulder and lightly squeezed. More than anything the man could have said to him, the gesture made Edane's throat tighten.

The bustle behind him faded into a hollow echo. As Broden left the hall, Edane stared down into Nellie's pale, unmoving face. The other ladies had not taken this long to revive.

Had he been wrong about her?

"No," he muttered as angry tears brimmed in his eyes. He shook his head, scattering them. "No," he said, louder. "The lass 'twas no demoness, for the Sluath didnae have her heart. 'Tis the most human thing we possess. I ken because she gave hers to me." He bent down over her, clutching her to his chest. "If you'll no' come to me," he whispered next to her ear, "then I must follow you."

"Jeepers," said a small hoarse voice, "I thought we quit trying to kill ourselves."

For a moment, Edane didn't move. But then he jerked upright and stared down as Nellie's eyelashes fluttered open. She looked up at him with a drowsy smile.

Joy flooded through Edane as a crazy grin spread over his face. "'Twould seem you're immortal now, my lady."

"How jake is that?" She winked. "Only had to shoot me. Three times."

For several long moments Edane could only look at her, as though turning away his gaze might undo what had been done. But someone cleared his throat, and Edane reluctantly looked up to see Kiaran watching them.

He nodded to the falconer, who approached and bowed to Nellie.

"I said to you much I now regret, Mistress Quinn. You saved my life, when I cared naught for yours. But for your sacrifice, I... Please forgive me." When the chieftain approached, smiling at them, the falconer turned to him. "I knew the lady left the stronghold in the night, but I told no one. I didnae care what happened to her."

"Indeed." All the good humor fled from Domnall's face. "You failed me sorely, Brother."

Kiaran nodded. "If you wish me gone, I shall leave in the morning."

"Now, wait a minute," Nellie said as she sat up. "Sorry, Chieftain. I'd just like to say something before you decide to kick him out."

Domnall eyed the falconer, and then nodded to her.

"Dun Chaill or the Gods or I don't know just gave me another chance to live, right?" She smiled at Edane. "After everything I did wrong the first time, too. Besides finding Danny, I think that's the best thing that's ever happened to me. Everyone should have a second chance." She regarded Kiaran, a little glint of satisfaction in her eyes. "Just remember, I gave you yours."

Respect warmed his cool eyes, and the falconer bowed to her.

"Your words have weight, Mistress Quinn," the chieftain said. "You may stay, Kiaran. Only ken that 'tis your last chance."

Chapter Thirty-Nine

※

CUL DRANK LISTLESSLY from a stolen bottle of whiskey as he listened to the voices in the great hall. The touch-reader had been revived, and another escaped slave rescued. Mariena Douet's particular gift held no interest for him, although her vicious nature amused him. How the Mag Raith would enjoy learning of her past.

He could still smell the ash of the fallen on his flesh, but he'd been obliged to remain cloaked until the battle had concluded. Many demons had died, so many that he'd dared hope to see the prince among them. But Iolar had been too shrewd again, using his pet druid to escape unscathed.

Cul finished the whiskey before he trudged down the tunnels toward his chamber. The sound of two voices murmuring drew him to the new listening post he'd built by tunneling under the greenhouse to place it beyond the reach of the shaman's wards.

The Mag Raith thought themselves clever, and indeed they were. Just not clever enough.

Chapter Forty

EDANE INSISTED ON taking Nellie out to the greenhouse to speak alone to her. When she came in, she saw their makeshift bed still there and laughed.

"Is that why you brought me out here? Not this time, Mister." She poked him in the chest. "I want to make love in a real bed. Not on the floor, in the grass, or in the rain." She sidled up against him. "At least, not tonight."

"Aye." He linked his hands behind her waist. "In the storm, I demanded much of you. You drive me mad sometimes. Forgive me that."

"Ah, heat of the moment." Nellie shrugged. "I'm not a delicate flower. I only look like one." She stroked his jaw with her fingers. "Besides, I like you when you're demanding."

"You smell like flowers. You taste…" His mouth came down on hers for a moment. "…like honey and sunshine. I love you, and I ken you love me, so I must ask properly now. Will you mate with me, my lady? Will you be my wife, and share your eternity with me?"

Nellie pressed her cheek against his heart, and listened to the steady beat of it for moment. She thought of all the wisecracks she could make, but that was the old Nellie. For the woman she chose to be, it just came down to two words.

"I will."

Sneak Peek

Broden (Immortal Highlander, Clan Mag Raith Book 4)

Excerpt

CHAPTER ONE

STANDING IN THE shadows of Dun Chaill's great hall, Broden mag Raith watched Mariena Douet sleep. Firelight painted her with glowing colors, tinting the porcelain paleness of her hair and skin. Even from where he stood, he could smell the rain-washed headiness of her scent, like angelica after a storm. Absent expression, her face appeared calm, almost serene—yet her hands remained in loose fists. Blood flecked some of her fingers and stained the inside of one thin wrist.

Gazing upon her yet felt as if Broden had somehow gone mad.

For weeks he'd dreamt of this female, in both tantalizing detail and frustrating uncertainty. In hours of slumber, he'd held and kissed and caressed her, giving and taking pleasures with her that only the most ardent lovers shared. For all the females he'd lain with over his long life, he'd never felt such a consuming passion. He would have happily spent eternity in her arms, feasting on her as a sumptuous, unending banquet. Each time he awoke he felt addled, and almost convinced she could not be flesh.

Tonight, she'd dropped from the sky in the aftermath of a battle between his clan and the demonic Sluath, as if a victory boon from the Gods. But that illusion had lasted until the moment the lady had awakened.

In Broden's dreams he'd looked upon Mariena as if through eyes filled with rain, so that she seemed only a blur of pale hair and skin. Now he could see everything of her, from a tousled mane of white and light gold to the thin, arched elegance of her bare feet. Since she had arrived naked after escaping the demons, nothing of her provided a hint of what time she had been taken from by the Sluath. Her features, more handsome than pretty, appeared as young and innocent as any maiden's.

Her quickness and surety an hour past had banished that notion as well.

Edane, the clan's shaman-trained archer, finished his examination of the unconscious lady. He covered her with a wool blanket, taking care to cover her bare feet. He then scrubbed a hand over his long scarlet hair as he beheld her another moment.

"No wounds or bruising, thank the Gods," he told Domnall, the Mag Raith clan's chieftain. "'Tis likely she'll wake calmer once she's rested. Only dinnae be fooled by her look of frailty. That swan's skin covers muscles as fit and hard as a man's."

"Aye, and she fights as one." The big man regarded his mate. "This French tongue the lady first spoke, 'tis common in your time, Wife?"

"In France, Canada, and most of Europe,

but not in my country." Jenna Cameron had come to the clan in fourteenth-century Scotland, but had been abducted from twenty-first century America, where she had worked as an architect. "Miss Douet used English with some fluency, and Rosealise speaks French like a native, so we shouldn't have any problem communicating with her."

No one mentioned the other reason they might expect difficulty with Mariena. Broden wondered if they thought it a kindness to him. He said nothing, aware as always that while his looks had always been called god-like, the sound of his harsh, damaged voice rasped unpleasantly in everyone's ears.

"One more thing," Jenna said, touching the chieftain's arm. "Her face looks familiar to me. I'm pretty sure that she escaped the underworld with the rest of us."

Domnall glanced at Broden, a flicker of sympathy in his green eyes before he said to his wife, "You should change into something dry, my love."

"We both need a bath first," she said. The slender, dark-haired architect glanced down at her mud-spattered garments. "Before I hit the showers, I'll check on Nellie and Rosealise. They were both pretty shaken up by, ah, mademoiselle's introduction." She gave Broden a rueful look before she left the hall.

All gentleness left Domnall's expression as he regarded the two men. "You and Edane secure the hall so the lady cannae set fires or run loose. Mael has the keepe watch until dawn, and I the next. Kiaran isnae in any shape to relieve us, so sleep while you may." He headed after his wife.

Moving heavy stones to block the doorways provided welcome occupation for Broden, even with the odd weakness that had beset him since the battle. He then watched from the kitchens as Edane cast protective spells over the hearths and torches. When the archer stepped through to join him, Broden shifted the last blocks into place, effectively turning the hall into a spacious prison.

Through a gap in the stones he peered in at Mariena, only to assure himself that she still slept. When he turned around, he saw Edane bring out his box of medicines.

"I thought Kiaran but muddled by the

spell blast," Broden said, disuse rendering his voice little more than a grinder of words.

"'Tis no' for the falconer," the archer said, nodding toward his throat. "You yet bleed."

Touching the new wound atop the old scar on his throat, Broden took away his fingers to find them spotted with thick, dark blood. Until this moment he'd felt no pain, but now it throbbed like a sore tooth. His hand also shook slightly, and he looked up to see Edane watching the tremor.

"Dinnae be a facking wench," the trapper told him flatly. "'Tis naught but weariness."

The archer nodded, and with silent speed attended to the deep cut, cleaning it before he applied a soothing salve. As he did Broden stared past him without seeing anything but Mariena's face. It seemed now permanently fixed in his mind.

"'Tis better," Edane said and stepped back. "'Twill want a bandage if 'tis still open in the morning." His blue eyes shifted to Broden's, and filled with doubt. "I should see how Kiaran fares before I seek my lady and our bed." He hesitated before he touched Broden's shoulder. "Dinnae brood longer,

Brother. I vow we'll fathom more on the morrow."

The trapper doubted that, and everything else now, but Edane would not leave him if he thought him addlepated. "My thanks, and fair night."

Once the archer left, Broden retrieved a bottle of whiskey from their stores and drank directly from it. Although as an immortal he could no longer become drunk, the burn of the spirit distracted him from the throb of his neck.

It did nothing to soothe the churn of his thoughts.

Handsome as he surely was, Broden had fared none too well with females. His own mother, a headman's bed slave, had died bearing him. Sileas, his sire's vengeful wife, had then tried to strangle the life from him, forcing her mate to foster Broden with another tribe. There, among the Mag Raith, the one Pritani lass he might have loved had been openly humiliated for opening her heart to a worthless slaveborn like him. The *dru-widess* lovers he'd since taken had offered their bodies, never their affections.

Since she had begun appearing in his dreams, his pale-haired lover had slowly become his one hope of happiness. She'd given herself to him again and again, holding nothing back, so generous and passionate a lover that he'd felt humbled. She'd whispered her love to him as well, her voice sweet and low as she'd lavished him with affection and devotion. To his mind, surely if she had given her heart to him so entirely when they'd been slaves in the Sluath underworld, then it would be so again when she found him. At long last he would have a mate of his own, a woman with whom he could share his life and his heart.

So she had come, too, as suddenly as the battle with the Sluath had ended.

Seeing her fall from the sky had near paralyzed Broden. She'd been so still at first, he'd thought her dead. He vaguely remembered falling to his knees in despair. Yet the Gods had not been so cruel as that. When he'd touched her, he'd felt her warmth, and the whispering pulse of her heart. He stroked his hand over her hair, feeling again the slippery weight of it. In his dreams the pale silk of it had veiled them as she'd kissed his throat, and spoken of her love.

Her love indeed.

Broden emptied half the bottle before he set the whiskey aside, and pressed his hand to his throat. Why the wound had not closed should have worried him. Thanks to the healing powers of his immortality he and the other Mag Raith hadn't suffered from a lasting injury in more than a thousand years.

From this ye cannae flee, Sileas's icy voice gloated from his memories.

• • • • •

Buy *Broden (Immortal Highlander, Clan Mag Raith Book 4)*

Glossary

Here are some brief definitions to help you navigate the medieval world of the Clan Mag Raith series, and also Nellie's Roaring Twenties Slang below.

Clan Mag Raith

amaro: a bittersweet herbal liqueur blended with gin and vermouth to make a Hanky-Panky cocktail
aquila: Latin for "eagle", the standard of a Roman legion
aulden: medieval slang for "archaic"
bairn: child
Banbury tale: Victorian slang for a nonsensical story

bannock: a round, flat loaf of unleavened Scottish bread
bloodwort: alternate name for yarrow
bloomers: Victorian word for "trousers"
blue-stocking: Victorian slang for "intellectual"
boak: Scottish slang for "vomit"
borage: alternate name for starflower (Borago officinalis)
broch: an ancient round hollow-walled structure found only in Scotland
burraidh: Scots Gaelic for "bully"
cac: Scots gaelic for "shit"
c'est bon: French for "it's good"
chanter: a woodwind instrument used alone as practice for playing the bagpipes
chebs: Scottish slang for "breasts"
conclave: druid ruling body
Cornovii: name by which two, or three, tribes were known in Roman Britain
cossetted: cared for in an overindulgent way
cottar: an agricultural worker or tenant given lodgings in return for work
Cuingealach: Scots Gaelic for "the narrow pass"
curate: a member of the clergy engaged as an assistant to a vicar, rector, or parish priest

deadfall trap: a type of trap fashioned to drop a heavy weight on the prey

deamhan (plural: *deamhanan*): Scots Gaelic for demon

dolabra: Latin for "pickaxe"

don't take any wooden nickels: early 20th century American slang for "don't do something stupid"

doss: leaves, moss, and other detritus covering the ground dru-wid: Proto Celtic word; an early form of "druid"

drystane: a construction of stacked stone or rock that is not mortared together

dunnage: Victorian slang for "clothing"

fash: feel upset or worried

fizzing: Victorian slang for "first-rate" or "excellent"

fletching: feathering an arrow

floorer: Victorian slang for "knocking someone down"

flummery: a custard-like Welsh dessert made from milk, beaten eggs and fruit

footman: a liveried servant whose duties include admitting visitors and waiting at table

forthright: honest

fortitude: courage under pressure

frittata: Italian egg dish similar to a crustless quiche

gainsay: contradict

give the sack: English slang for "firing someone from their job"

gladii: Latin plural of *gladius* or "sword"

glock: Victorian slang for "half-wit"

gongoozler: Victorian slang for "an idle, dawdling person"

goof: early 20th century American slang for "a man in love"

grice: a breed of swine found in the Highlands and Islands of Scotland and in Ireland

groat: a type of medieval silver coin worth approximately four pence

gu bràth: Scots Gaelic for forever, or until Judgment

Guédelon: a 25-year-long archaeological experiment in Treigny, France to recreate a 13th century castle

hold your wheesht: Scottish slang term for "maintaining silence and calm"

hoor: medieval slang for "whore", "prostitute"

Hussar: member of the light cavalry

in the scud: Scottish slang for "naked"

jem: Medieval Scots slang for a person prized for beauty and excellence, a "gem"

jess: a short leather strap that is fastened around each leg of a hawk

kirk: Scottish slang for "church"

*kithan:*Medieval Scots term for a "demon"

knacker: Victorian slang for "an old, useless horse"

laudanum: a tincture of opium

luaidh: Scots Gaelic for "loved one" or "darling"

mademoiselle: French for "Miss"

maister: medieval slang for "master" or "leader"

make a stuffed bird laugh: Victorian slang phrase for something that is "preposterous or contemptible"

máthair: Scots Gaelic for "mother"

nag: slang for horse

n'aie pas peur: French for ""Don't be afraid"

naught-man: an unearthly creature that only looks like a man

nock: the slotted end of an arrow that holds it in place on the bowstring

non: French for "no"

*nous sommes tes ami*s: French for "We are your

friends"
oui: French for "yes"
panay: alternate name for self-heal (*Prunella vulgaris*)
pantaloons: Victorian word for "trousers"
parti: the ideas or plans influencing an architect's design
peignoir: Victorian-era woman's garment similar to a "negligee or a light dressing gown"
peridot: a green semi-precious mineral, a variety of olivine
peyrl: Scots Gaelic for "pearl"
plumbata: lead-weighted throwing dart used by the Romans
pomatum: greasy, waxy, or water-based substance used to style hair
quern: a primitive hand mill for grinding grain made of two stones
reste en arriére: French for "Stay back"
rollicking: fun and boisterous
rooing: removing sheep's loose fleece by hand-pulling
sham: false, fake
sica: a long curved dagger
skeg: Scots Gaelic for "demon"
spend: ejaculate

stand hunt: to watch for prey from a blind or place of concealment
stele: an upright pillar bearing inscriptions
stockman: a person who looks after livestock
strewing: plants scattered on the floor as fragrance, insecticide, and disinfectant
tapachd: Scots Gaelic for "an ability of confident character not to be afraid or easily intimidated"
taverit: Scottish slang for "worn out, exhausted"
tear bottle: Used in the Victorian revival of the ancient custom of catching tears of mourning in a small vial with a loose stopper. When the bottled tears evaporated, the period of mourning was considered over.
touch-reader: a person with psychometric ability; someone who touch objects to envision their history
trigging: in stonework, using wedge pieces to secure a construct
treadwheel crane: a human-powered wooden wheeled device used for hoisting and lowering materials
trodge: Scottish slang for "trudge"
valise: a small traveling bag or suitcase

vous parlez anglaise: French for "Do you speak English?"

woundwort: alternate name for wound healer (*Anthyllis vulneraria*)

Roaring Twenties Slang

baby: a person (male or female)

ball-and-chain: spouse

bangtail: horse

bathtub swill: poor, cheaply-made liquor

beef: argument, conflict

bee's knees: a highly admired person or thing

behind the eight ball: in a difficult position

big cheese: man in charge, the boss

big sleep: death

bigshot: important person

blow: leave

body blankets: precursor to body bags

boob: idiot

breeze: leave

button man: hit man, killer for hire

buzz: looks for a person, comes to a person's door

cat's meow: splendid

chill off: murder

chippy: a loose woman with few or no morals

chump: a gullible person

clip: shoot

copper: law enforcement officer

dame: woman

dish: a pretty woman

dive: a low-class place

dizzy doll: clueless

do it up: party, drink, carouse

drill: shoot

droppers: hired killers

duck's quack: the best thing ever

duds: clothes

dump: dirty, disorganized, unattractive place

flapper: a fashionable, fun-loving young woman who defied conventional thinking and behavior

flatties: police

flim-flam: swindle, con job

floorflusher: an experienced dancer

floozy: an experienced promiscuous woman

get stuck on: have a crush on

gander: look

goon: bad guy, thug

gunned down: shot

Hanky-Panky: a cocktail created in 1925 by

Savoy bartender Ada Coleman

hatchet man: assassin

hinky: suspicious

hobo: drifter

hooch: liquor

hoof: dance

horse feathers: nonsense

Houdini: someone who is punctual

huffy: offended

in the altogether: naked

the cat's pajamas: something very good, excellent

jake: okay, fine

jam: trouble

Jeepers: a mild oath, a euphemism for Jesus

joint: place

kisser: face

kitty: female genitals

loony: insane

lug: a dull-witted man

make like the canary: inform to the police

making whoopee: having sex

maroon: a person who is easy to deceive

Mickey Finn: a drink doctored with knock-out drugs

mug: stupid man

ossified: drunk

out on the roof: dizzy, drunk

palooka: unintelligent man

peaches: breasts

peeve: annoy or upset

petting: kissing, caressing and touching

petting party: make-out session

plant: bury

plug: person

pro skirt: prostitute

Prohibition: From 1920 until 1933, a constitutional national ban on the production, importation, transportation and sale of alcoholic beverages in the United States

pug: boxer

pumped full of lead: shot multiple times

pushover: easy

put the finger on: blame

put the screws to: interrogate by force

put the squeeze on: coerce or intimidate

rags: clothes

rat out: inform on

ritzy: very elegant

rube: an easy mark

sap: dunce

score: the reckoning of a situation

scram: run away
shack: reside
shakes out: proven to happen
sharper: swindler
sheik: handsome, sexy man
skirt: woman
snitch: informant
song and dance: deception
sister: woman
skedaddle: leave quickly, run
speakeasy: a bar or nightclub that sold alcohol illegally during Prohibition
swank, swanky: elegant
tot: small child
trouble boys: gangsters
you slay me: you're hilarious
sap: hit
sitting pretty: to be in an ideal situation
smarts: hurts
spike: nail
squeeze: girlfriend
stickler: a person who always follows the rules
upsidaisy: a phrase said to reassure someone (usually a child) being lifted
wise guy: smart aleck
yammer: to speak loudly

Pronunciation Guide

A selection of the more challenging words in the Immortal Highlander, Clan Mag Raith series.

Aklen: ACK-lin
aquila: uh-KEE-lah
Bacchanalian: back-NIL-ee-ahn
bannock: BAN-ick
boak: BOWK
Bridget McMurphy: BRIH-jet mick-MER-fee
Broden mag Raith: BRO-din MAG RAYTH
burraidh: BURR-ee
cac: kak
Carac: CARE-ick
Clamhan: CLEM-en
Clarinda Gowdon: kler-IN-dah GOW-don

Cornovii: core-KNOW-vee-eye
Cuingealach: kwin-GILL-ock
Cul: CULL
Danar: dah-NAH
Dapper: DAH-purr
Darro: DAR-oh
deamhan: DEE-man
dolabra: dohl-AH-brah
Domnall mag Raith: DOM-nall MAG RAYTH
Dun Chaill: DOON CHAYLE
Eara: EER-ah
Edane mag Raith: eh-DAYN MAG RAYTH
Fargas: FAR-gus
Fiana: FEYE-eh-nah
Fraser: FRAY-zir
Frew: FREE
frittata: free-TAH-tah
Galan Aedth: gal-AHN EEDTH
gladii: GLAHD-ee-ee
groat: GROWT
gu bràth: GOO BRATH
Hal Maxwell: HOWL MACK-swell
Helen Frances Quinn: HELL-uhn FRAN-sess KWIN
Hussar: hoo-ZAHR

Iolar: EYE-el-er
Jackie Facelli: JA-kee fah-CHELL-ee
Jaeg: YEGG
jem: GEM
Jenna Cameron: JEHN-nah CAM-er-ahn
John McMurphy: JAWN mick-MER-fee
Kiaran mag Raith: KEER-ahn MAG RAYTH
kithan: KEY-tin
laudanum: LAH-deh-num
luaidh: LOO-ee
Lyle Gordon: lie-EL GORE-din
Mael mag Raith: MAIL MAG RAYTH
maister: MAY-ster
Mariena Douet: mah-REE-nah DOO-eh
marster: MAR-stir
Mary Gowdon: MARE-ee GOW-don
máthair: muh-THERE
Meirneal: MEER-nee-el
Michael Patrick Quinn: MYK-uhl PAH-treek KWIN
Mickie: MIH-kee
Nectan: NECK-tin
Nellie: NELL-ee
parti: PAR-tee
peignoir: pen-WAH
peyrl: PEH-rill

plumbata: PLOOM-bah-tah
pomatum: pah-MADE-uhm
quern: KWERN
Rodney Percell: RAHD-knee purr-SELL
Rosealise Dashlock: roh-see-AH-less DASH-lock
Seabhag: SHAH-vock
Serca: SAIR-eh-kah
sica: SEE-kah
Sileas: SIGH-lee-ess
skeg: SKEHG
Sluath: SLEW-ahth
tapachd: TAH-peed
taverit: tah-VAIR-eet
tisane: TEE-zahn
trodge: TRAHJ
valise: vuh-LEES
Wachvale: WATCH-veil
wheesht: WEESHT

Dedication

For Mr. H.

Copyright

Copyright © 2019 Hazel Hunter

This is a work of fiction. Names, characters, places, and incidents are products of the author's imagination or are used fictitiously and are not to be construed as real. Any resemblance to actual events, locales, organizations, or persons, living or dead, is coincidental.

All rights reserved. No part of this book may be used or reproduced in any manner, stored in or introduced into a retrieval system, or transmitted, in any form, or by any means (electronic, mechanical, photocopying, recording, or otherwise), without the prior written consent of the copyright owner.

The scanning, uploading, and distribution of this book via the Internet or via any other means without the permission of the copyright owner is illegal. Please purchase only authorized electronic editions, and do not participate in or encourage electronic piracy of copyrighted materials. Your support of the author's rights is appreciated.

CPSIA information can be obtained
at www.ICGtesting.com
Printed in the USA
LVHW080141110420
653065LV00017B/330